PLAIN TROUBLE

ALISON STONE

D1528299

TREEHAVEN PRESS

PLAIN TROUBLE
Treehaven Press
Copyright © 2021 by Alison Stone

This book is a work of fiction. The names, characters, places, and incidents
are products of the writer's imagination or have been used fictitiously and
are not to be construed as real. Any resemblance to persons, living or dead,
actual events, locale or organizations is entirely coincidental.

Be the first to learn about new books, giveaways, and deals by signing up for
Alison's newsletter on her website: https://alisonstone.com/newsletter

❀ Created with Vellum

CHAPTER 1

*H*ope Baker stuffed the last tablecloth into the sack and tossed it over her shoulder. "Oof," she grunted as the heavy bag landed solidly on her back. Rolling her shoulders, she peeked through the slit in the door leading to the large dining room/living room combination. The guest of honor's husband carried the last of their haul out the door. He seemed like a good man. Hope prayed he was, for his new wife's sake. Hope had found out the hard way that a person didn't always know another person's heart until it was too late. From what Hope overheard—she didn't like to think of herself as the type of person who would eavesdrop, but she was still trying to figure things out in Hunters Ridge, and a person got a lot of information from lingering in the background and keeping her ears open—this mother-to-be had already had her share of heartache.

Hope tried not to feel bad about listening to all the gossip. She had been the subject of it more times than she cared to count and it made her skin crawl, especially because a lot of it was mean, hurtful…untrue. She had escaped the worst of it, managing to arrive in town a month ago, land this job, and pretty much stay under the radar.

"You don't have to go to the laundromat now. It's late."

Hope spun around to find Mrs. Lapp standing in the kitchen behind her. *Mary.* Hope adjusted the handle of the bag slung over her shoulder. "I don't mind." She figured she'd have the place to herself.

"Save it until Monday." Tomorrow was Sunday and her Amish boss would be keeping the sabbath. The laundromat would be closed, as would most other stores in the small town.

"I'd rather get it done tonight. Monday will bring its own share of chores." Hope smiled. She enjoyed the mundaneness of some tasks that allowed her a few quiet moments. She had a good book in her tote bag that she had been anxious to get back to. Saturday-night laundry sounded like a dream.

"I hadn't realized the baby shower would go so late," Mary said by way of an apology. But they both knew she was happy to have the business. Running a B&B in a small town apparently wasn't very lucrative, even though they were well into the leaf-peeper season.

And Hope was grateful for the job. Mary had offered it to her almost immediately upon learning she needed one. Hope feared the woman was just being nice so she wanted to make herself useful so she wouldn't change her mind. However, working in a B&B wouldn't have been Hope's first choice because each new guest brought the fear that someone might recognize her as Harper Miller from the suburbs of Buffalo. A woman who needed to stay missing.

Hope—she had trained herself to think of herself by that name, for fear she'd slip up or not respond to someone's call (which had happened far more times than she cared to admit) —hadn't been able to see the evil until it was almost too late.

Almost.

2

Her tongue touched her bottom lip, a subconscious gesture whenever she thought of the beating she had taken. She shoved the thoughts aside. She was here. Alive. Out of reach.

New name. New hair color. New life.

"Would you like company?" Mary asked. "I'm not sure how I feel about you going into town so late. Alone. I'm sure Ada wouldn't mind going with you."

Eighteen-year-old Ada was Mary's youngest child, the only one not yet married off. They'd started the B&B two years ago after Mary's husband died and farming became too difficult. Mary seemed suited to it and Ada was chatty and generally agreeable with all the guests.

"It's eight p.m. in Hunters Ridge." Hope tried to sound like Mary's concern was the most ridiculous thing she had ever heard. The string of the laundry bag dug into her shoulder, so she plunked it down at her feet. "Ada should stay here. She can help you tidy up." Hope smiled and hoisted the bag but didn't throw it over her shoulder this time. "I've got this."

"If you're sure."

"I am."

Mary pressed her lips together, seeming resigned. "Make sure you take your cell phone and call if you need anything. It's so dark out already."

"Will do." Even if Hope called, it was unlikely Mary would hear the phone ring all the way out in the barn. The Amish had interesting ways to get around the rules.

She pushed open the door and bumped the laundry bag out onto the porch. She ran back inside and grabbed the burner phone she had purchased. For emergencies only. She didn't plan to have any this evening.

Or ever again, if she had her way.

The husband from earlier had returned after loading up the baby gifts into his truck. The soon-to-be new parents who had just married had rented a room for the night. Mary would set out a buffet and Hope would make sure they had fresh coffee and anything else they needed while the mother-daughter team were at Sunday service.

"Need some help with that?" he asked when he apparently saw her widen her stance to steady herself.

"Nah, I'm good." Hope tightened her grip and took a step down the porch.

He tilted his head. "Humor me."

Hope had overheard that the baby was actually her new husband's dead brother's, but the brother had died tragically. When the surviving brother came to town to find out what happened to his brother, his brother's widow and he fell in love. Now they'd be raising the baby. It was definitely the fodder for rumor mills, and Hope hated that she knew all this information about him. It seemed like an invasion of privacy, but his wide smile and kind eyes suggested he didn't have a care in the world. Not today, anyway.

Hope set the laundry down and rocked back on her heels, adjusting the small tote bag with her book and phone on her shoulder. "I'm in that van. The work one." She gestured to the white van with the B&B logo on it, an outline of a farmhouse and an Amish buggy. She jogged ahead and opened the door. The man placed the laundry inside the back. "Thanks."

"You're welcome." He waved, walking backward. "Have a good night."

"You, too. I suppose I'll see you in the morning. Be sure to let me know if you need anything."

"Will do."

She watched him jog back into the B&B where he'd join his wife and celebrate all their good fortune. A new marriage. A baby.

A fresh wave of loneliness washed over her. She stood frozen, staring at the pretty farmhouse. The evening's illumi-

4

nation gave the structure a warm glow. A generator had been installed for the convenience of the guests and because it wasn't connected to the grid, Mary avoided running afoul of the *Ordnung*. Another way to show how clever the Amish were when it came to getting around some of the rules. Inside, her benefactor was mopping the kitchen floor. Hope would do laundry ten times over mopping. A stiff wind whipped up and rustled the fine hairs that had escaped her neat braid. She glanced around to a darkness never achieved in the city. Only in the day could she see the field that had once grown corn and the thick woods beyond it. But now it was as black as the basement closet her ex once held her in.

Is someone out there?

Stop. She was safe. No one from her past knew she was in Hunters Ridge.

A surge of adrenaline made her rush to the driver's side of the van, yank open the door and climb in. At first it'd seemed odd that Mary owned a vehicle, because she didn't drive. But it soon became clear she was a smart business-woman who could find workarounds. Little Amos, a young Amish man who didn't blink at being called in the diminutive despite standing at six feet, had yet to be baptized so the church leadership didn't seem to frown on him taking odd jobs as a driver. And now Hope was available to do the same.

Once safely inside the van, Hope adjusted the radio to her favorite Top 40 station. She had missed the ability to stream whatever music she wanted whenever she wanted, but she decided this was a small price to pay for anonymity and peace of mind. She respected her employer and was willing to play by the rules for a job, which meant no technology that the Amish couldn't use. Except in her case, the van and cell phone. And they were careful not to abuse the benefits of a generator.

Hope liked to believe her own dead mother had found

her this job because it was a photo of her mother, Mary Lapp and Hope as a young girl on a trip to see the Amish that had brought her back here more than a decade later. Hope had always sensed the trip to Hunters Ridge held some significance for her mother, but sadly she passed a few months later without sharing what that might have been. However Mary claimed that a lot of tourists took her photo—which was against the *Ordnung*—so Hope let it drop, not wanting to offend the Amish woman who had so willingly taken her in. Feeling nostalgic about the last summer with her mother, Hope kept the photo pressed between the pages of whatever book she was currently reading.

Hope had always found herself deep in thought when she drove. An animal of some sort darted into the fringes of her headlights and scooted just as quickly back into the fields that lined the dark country road, snapping her back into the moment with a jolt from tapping her brakes. Her heart raced and she flicked on the high beams and reduced her speed. She had heard horrible stories about deer jumping out and causing major accidents. The last thing she needed was to end up in some hospital, with no insurance, under an assumed name. Shoulders tense, palms slicked, and nerves rattled, she arrived at the Wash & Go on Main Street and tried to remind herself that a few minutes of quiet would be worth the drive.

Hope parked on the street in front of the laundromat and gathered her things quickly and rushed inside. She wasn't exactly safe. Sure, the lights were bright, but anyone could come in. And there was no one else around.

She tossed the laundry bag down next to a washing machine and dug for coins in her tote. That was what he had taken from her. Her sense of safety. Freedom. Even her identity. She had to force herself beyond her limited comfort zone to convince herself someday she'd work her way back to normal. Someday.

Whenever that was.

Despite the warm autumn evening, there was a chill in the air that followed her into the building. She should have grabbed her hoodie. She stuffed the tablecloths into three washers and started them up.

She settled into a hard plastic chair with her back to the window. The fluorescent lights emitted a constant low buzz that could be heard above the *whoosh-whoosh-whoosh* of the washer. She opened the book and stared at the words but couldn't focus. She slid out the photo of her, her mother and Mary. Mary had always looked distracted in the photo, perhaps simply because she was unwilling to tell the tourist that it was forbidden to take her photo.

Yet young Hope had a silly smile on her face while her mother's expression seemed anxious. For years, Hope had created an imaginary dialogue between the women, but it turned out they were strangers.

The memory evoked an unsettling feeling and the fine hairs on the back of her neck prickled to life. Hope glanced over her shoulder. Her hollowed-out expression stared back at her in the cloudy window. Across the street, the open sign on a small shop went dark.

She tilted her head from side to side, trying to ease the knot that was tightening between her shoulder blades. Unable to sit still, she got up and wandered the rows of washers and dryers. She had been here twice before to do her own laundry. She went to the bulletin board and read a notice for an available apartment. Maybe when she saved enough, she'd be able to get a place of her own. For now, she was grateful for Mary Lapp's generosity, providing a bedroom, one too small to rent out to overnight guests of the B&B.

Something tickled the far reaches of her brain and then grew louder. *Sirens.* All the blood drained from her face. The urge to flee nearly overwhelmed her, making her feel nauseous.

It's fine. It's fine. No one knows you're here.

The sirens grew louder. She moved to the back of the laundromat, away from the large windows.

No one knows you're here.

She sat down on the worn linoleum, leaning against a row of washing machines, and buried her head in her hands.

You're fine. You're fine.

The sound of racing engines grew closer with the persistent wail of the sirens. Tires screeched. Glass smashed. Metal skidding across dated linoleum.

Her entire body bumped forward. She threw down her hands and scrambled like a crab dumped from the net onto the deck of a fishing boat.

A scream ripped from her lips.

The lights flickered, then went off.

Trembling, she stood. Ignoring the shards of glass that had rained down on her, she turned around.

A pickup truck had crashed into the storefront, narrowly missing her. She held up her hand to block the blinding headlights. The driver's head was tipped forward against the steering wheel.

"Oh my..." she whispered; her entire mouth had gone dry. She picked her way through the broken glass, around the displaced washers, and over to the driver's side door.

"Step back!" a voice shouted from outside on the sidewalk.

Hope shifted, the glass crunching under her sneakers, to find a sheriff's deputy aiming a gun at her. Instinctively she held up her hands and fought the tears filling her eyes. Her

8

heart thundered in her chest, making it difficult to comprehend the deputy's commands.

"I was doing laundry," she squeaked out, realizing even in that moment how ridiculous she sounded. "I didn't do anything wrong."

The deputy made his way into the destroyed storefront. The barely contained anger on his face made her flash back to her ex. The hatred in the eyes was all too familiar.

"Ma'am, are you okay?" he asked.

She swallowed and only mustered a nod.

"You'll need to step back," he ordered.

Hope complied on shaky legs.

The deputy slipped past her and yanked open the truck door. Still aiming his gun at the man. "Put your hands where I can see them."

The driver lifted his head and tilted it back on the headrest. A sly smile slanted his lips as he lifted his hands and slapped them down on the steering wheel. "Are you going to shoot me?" His speech was slurred. If it weren't for the trickle of blood running down his forehead and cheek, he might have passed for someone waking up from a deep sleep. A sarcastic someone.

What's going on? she wondered as she tried to make sense of the scene.

Be brave, another voice whispered.

Hope stepped forward. "Doesn't he need medical attention?"

The deputy blinked, seeming to snap out of it. Just then, another deputy rushed in. "Let me take over. You see to the woman." The new deputy on the scene glanced around with wide eyes. "Anyone else in here?"

"No, no…I was doing laundry alone."

The deputy held out his palm. "Let's go outside where I can ask you some questions."

Alarm spiked her heart rate. Questions? She didn't want to have to lie to this man. But more than that, she didn't want her name in an official report that her ex could track.

Hope Baker had only recently settled into a new town and job. She didn't want to have to run again.

CHAPTER 2

*D*eputy Travis Hart scanned the destruction his brother-in-law, Kerry Turner, had brought down on Wash & Go. The blinding rage pulsing in his head made it nearly impossible to think straight. "Stand over there, ma'am. I'll be right with you." He turned his back to the woman who had probably just had the shock of her life.

With trembling hands, Travis dialed his sister's cell phone for the second time. No answer. She wasn't one of those people glued to her phone, so he shouldn't worry. But he did. Her husband had plowed into the front of the building and reeked of alcohol.

Travis wanted to go back into the building and drag his brother-in-law out of the truck but let Deputy Kimble do the honors. It was better for everyone.

"Let go of me!" Kerry hollered belligerently. "I didn't do nothing."

If his declaration wasn't so darned ridiculous and his actions so dangerous, Travis might have laughed in his face. His recklessness could have killed someone.

Kimble nodded in Travis's direction, as if to say, *I got him.*

Travis was embarrassed to be related to this man, and his fellow deputy knew as much. It was a small town, after all.

Travis glanced at his cell phone screen. His sister hadn't returned his call. He tried again with no luck and cursed under his breath. If Kerry had done anything to his sister, he'd find him in his cell tonight and administer the throat punch the man deserved. Kerry had been known to abuse his sister, but his sister always forgave him and welcomed him back into their home. It was maddening. She claimed it was because of their son. But no kid deserved to live in such turmoil.

As Kimble ushered Kerry out of the debris, Travis asked, "Where's Ginny?" His sister couldn't have married a bigger loser. However, if he was feeling generous, he'd acknowledge that neither of them was a drug addict—that he knew—at the time of their marriage. And he wasn't feeling generous.

"I don't give a crap where she is." Kerry leaned forward, trying to spit on Travis, but the other deputy yanked him back by the forearm.

Kerry's hands were cuffed behind his back, making him a perfect target for that throat punch. But Travis wasn't that kind of person no matter how much fury pulsed in his head. If he had been, he'd be no better than too many men in his life.

"Do you care about your son?" Travis asked, swallowing the bile at the back of his throat.

"He's a whiny kid like his mother." A stone-cold expression flashed in his brother-in-law's spacey, bloodshot eyes. These were not the mutterings of a stoned drug addict. He meant every word of it. Aiden didn't deserve it. Any of it.

Travis fisted his free hand, then forced it to relax. He was not going to let this jerk take him down, too. He had worked too hard to get where he was. Unlike his sister, Travis wasn't inclined to follow this man down a dark path. Maybe this would be the pivotal moment that would make his sister finally say enough was enough, but he doubted it. The enough should have come five years ago at the birth of his nephew.

Poor kid had been dealt a cruel hand with those two as parents.

"Take this punk out of my sight." Travis turned and let out a long breath, trying to regain his cool. *Don't get distracted by all the garbage that keeps you awake at night. It's not worth it. Not right now.*

The woman who had been in the Wash & Go at the time of the accident cleared her throat, reminding him that she was still there. "Um, can someone take me home?"

For the first time since his brother-in-law led him on a high-speed chase that ended here, he looked at this woman. Really looked at her. He knew most people in town, but he didn't recognize her, and she'd be hard to miss. She had captivating blue eyes, porcelain skin with faint freckles, and a pretty shade of brown hair with red highlights pulled tight into a long braid. And despite the relatively mild night, she was shivering. "First, let's have the paramedics check you out." He held out his palm but didn't touch her.

Her eyes widened and she took a step backward. "I'm fine, really." She shook her head. "I need a ride. That's all."

"Well…" He waited, hoping to draw her gaze. When that didn't work, he forced a smile. He probably hadn't made the best impression while dealing with Kerry. He should have been more professional. "I'll need your information."

"I don't see why? I was in the wrong place at the wrong time."

She bit her bottom lip and he followed her gaze past the tail end of Kerry's red pickup truck. The blue W from the store's sign was sitting in the bed of the truck but it looked more like a lowercase epsilon. Her attention was focused on the smashed front end of what looked like a catering van.

"Is that yours?"

"Um, the woman I work for." Her pale coloring had him worried she was about to faint. "I'm not sure how she's going to afford to replace it."

"I'm sure your boss will understand." He pointed toward the ambulance but didn't risk touching her. She seemed skittish. "Let's go over here and talk. I'd like the paramedics to take a look at you."

She finally lifted her pale blue eyes to his face. Something flittered in their depths that he recognized from his five years in the sheriff's department. She was trying to get away without giving him any information.

Strange.

"You're not in trouble." He forced a laugh. "Unless you were the one who drove through the front of the building."

"No." The steely tone in that single word suggested she wasn't in the mood for joking.

"Hey Travis, I'm going to send this guy to the hospital," the other deputy hollered over. "He's complaining of a headache."

Travis did his best not to roll his eyes. He hated that he couldn't find compassion for his brother-in-law. Did people choose to become addicts?

"You get a hold of your sister?" the deputy asked as he hopped into the ambulance to escort Kerry. It wouldn't have been the first time a criminal used the "I'm hurt" excuse to jackrabbit out of the ER.

"Not yet." Travis checked his cell phone again. Nothing. His stomach sank. He dreaded giving his sister bad news, but his mounting fear was for his sister's well-being. Did an argument with Ginny precede Kerry hopping into his pickup and racing along the country roads? Had he done something to her? It wouldn't be the first time.

Travis turned back to the woman, suddenly growing impatient to check on his sister. "Name."

"Um..." She cleared her throat.

What's up with the hesitation?

"You do have a name, don't you?" he teased, even though he was far from being in a playful mood. He immediately realized his mistake when her expression grew shuttered.

"I'm fine," she said, pressing her shoulders back. "I don't want to get checked out by the paramedics. I want to go home and get cleaned up." This was the most she had spoken since he found her in the wrecked store.

Kimble jerked his chin toward them. "Have her sign a release if she doesn't want to get checked out."

"Would you mind?" Travis asked.

The woman sighed heavily. "Yes, I'll sign your form."

Travis led her over to his patrol car and grabbed his laptop from the center console. He pulled up the doc and looked up at her. "You never gave me a name.

"Hope. My name is Hope," she finally said, seemingly angry that he had forced it out of her. He didn't understand why.

"Last name."

"Baker."

He entered the information on the form. She seemed to grow twitchy when she gave him the address of the B&B where she appeared to live as well as work.

When he was done, he snapped the laptop closed. "Do you have someone to call for a ride?"

Hope sighed heavily. "No, I don't have anyone to call." Her agitation was palpable. She glanced around, as if debating the alternatives.

"If you don't mind waiting a few minutes until the owner

gets here, then I can drive you home myself." After that he'd swing by Ginny's place to check on her. Unless she called him first.

Hope shrugged, looking like she was holding back tears. Travis understood that the young woman had suffered a shock, but something seemed off. She appeared hesitant, afraid, or maybe she was hiding something.

CHAPTER 3

*P*acing on the sidewalk, Hope kept shooting glances at the workers boarding up the smashed windows of the laundromat. They were almost done. She should have been thanking her lucky stars she hadn't been crushed under the truck while minding her own business washing tablecloths, but all she could think about was how she had to find another ride home. She did not want to get into a patrol car with the handsome deputy.

Good grief, what did it matter if he was easy on the eyes? Perhaps she had been lonelier than she realized, tucked upstairs in the closet-size bedroom away from her friends in Buffalo.

Ha—her ex, Derek, had already seen to the end of those friendships in a textbook case of isolating his victim. Yet she had been too blind to see it until she woke up one morning and realized she was one-too-many tequilas away from him losing it on her and ending her life.

The deputy was discussing something with the owner of the laundromat, allowing Hope to study him unobserved. Could she trust him? She wasn't sure what she was looking for. He had a neat haircut, short in the back and a little longer on top. Stylish, unlike her ex who preferred a basic buzz using a number one clipper guard. She knew because he made her learn how to use a trimmer after the "stupid airhead" at the salon nicked his ear. God help Hope if she didn't create a perfectly clean line at the back of his head. He made her hold up the mirror so he could check, then mocked her when her hands shook. A familiar anger bubbled to the surface. Man, she hated him. Hated what he had made her become.

Travis turned sideways and she quickly averted her gaze, but not before noting the hard set of his jaw had a five o'clock shadow. She'd guess he was about thirty. Five years older than she was. His broad shoulders filled out his jacket, and he kept shifting his stance and glancing at his phone. Something besides this mess demanded his attention. So she wasn't the only one on edge. She allowed herself to check out his left hand. No ring, but that meant nothing. Some men didn't wear jewelry. Did she think if he was married, she'd be safer? Did a long-term relationship prevent Derek from cheating? *Stop.*

Hope was in survival mode and overanalyzing everything. She would accept the deputy's ride. She had no choice. She prayed the sheriff's department wouldn't be asking her any more questions about the accident tonight. The fewer people she engaged with, the better.

Hope drew in a deep breath and let it out. An evening breeze rustled the leaves of the trees that lined Main Street, and that persistent uneasiness welled up and had her searching the street. What would it take for her to ever feel safe again?

The phone in her tote bag vibrated and it took a minute before she tuned into it. She dropped one handle off her shoulder and dug it out. "Hello?"

"Hope, it's Mary." The dear woman always sounded so formal over the phone. Hope had heard her make a few business calls from the barn, and she rarely made small talk, as if using the phone was such a breach of the *Ordnung* that she'd do her business and hang up immediately. "Is everything okay? It's getting late."

Hope placed the palm of her hand on her forehead at the sound of the familiar voice, relief easing the knot between her shoulder blades. "Yes, yes, I'm okay." Her voice cracked now that she was talking to someone who cared about her. How pathetic was she? She had only known this woman for a short time and she was practically weepy with relief that Mary had reached out to her. "However, there was an accident."

"Oh dear."

Hope could imagine the woman slowly lowering herself into a chair at the small table set up in the barn and wringing her hands. That was how she seemed to work her plans: staring off into the distance and twisting, twisting, twisting her hands. This had made Hope think the dear woman was genuinely stressed when Hope first came to her with photographic evidence that they had met before on an earlier visit to Hunters Ridge. Mary claimed she didn't remember the meeting, but her big heart extended an offer of a place to live and a job before Hope had a chance to finish her coffee and chocolate cream pie.

"I'm fine, but sadly, the van is not." Hope turned back at the sound of a diesel engine idling. The tow truck had arrived. "I'm really sorry. Someone hit it while it was parked in front of the laundromat."

"Possessions can be replaced," Mary said with an air of decisiveness. "I had no business tempting myself with such fancy things."

Hope found herself smiling, the first time since the

horrible sound of screeching and metal crunching had sent her scrambling at the laundromat. Mary Lapp was hardly the only one to fall prey to a temptation from the outside world. Hope hadn't known much about the Amish, but she was quickly learning. "They're towing the van now. Is there someplace special you'd like me to have them take it?"

"I wouldn't know. Little Amos takes care of those things." She made a quiet noise with her lips, as if she were weighing her options. "Somewhere close in town would work." What sounded like ruffling papers floated over the phone line.

Little Amos was the young man Mary employed to do what she termed "man's work." Hope did her best to hide her annoyance at the woman's sexist term, understanding Mary had grown up Amish and this was the way of life for them.

"I have to go," Hope said into the phone, then turned her attention to the tow truck driver who was working a mechanism to tilt the flatbed.

He stopped and walked over to her smelling of diesel and cigarette smoke. "This yours?" he asked, then plucked the cigarette out from between his lips with soiled cotton gloves.

She nodded and he handed her a business card.

"Call this garage in the morning and ask for Russ." Half his mouth quirked into a grin. "That's me. We'll know more about the extent of the damage."

"Thanks." She stuffed the card into the back pocket of her jeans. She hated that she had brought this mess down on Mary Lapp. As it was, the Amish woman barely seemed to have enough funds to keep the bed-and-breakfast operational. Yet her generosity hadn't allowed her to turn Hope away when she obviously needed a place to stay and a job.

The handsome deputy shook the hand of the tow truck driver, then turned to her. "Ready? I'll run you home."

Hope glanced around, looking for an escape route. She shouldn't let him know where she lived.

He doesn't know who you really are.

He doesn't know your ex.

You're safe. You're safe. You're safe. She had repeated that mantra in bed most nights when the creaks of the old farmhouse had gotten to be too much for her fried nerves.

"Ready?" The deputy tilted his head and seemed to be studying her with warm brown eyes. They were kind eyes, not like her ex's.

Heaven help me.

Hope snapped out of her spiraling thoughts and, based on the perplexed expression on his face, he must have asked her the question more than once. "Um, yeah." She was being silly. The name of her employer was emblazoned on the side of the dented van. He'd know where to find her even if she stubbornly refused his ride. "Are you sure you don't mind? I could call…" *Who could I call, really?*

"Come on." Travis tipped his head toward the patrol car parked across the street.

"You know where the bed-and-breakfast is on Route 321?"

"Sure, I know the place."

They walked over and he opened the back door. She froze for a heartbeat and felt panic well inside her. Once Derek had made her get into the back of his cruiser—as punishment—and left her there overnight in their garage, trapped. With her pulse roaring in her ears, Hope locked eyes with this stranger and the world seemed to shift around her.

It's okay. You're safe. You're safe.

Apparently sensing her misgivings, the deputy said, "I'm sorry, I have a lot of stuff on the front passenger seat." He smiled.

He exuded warmth, but she didn't trust herself when it came to men. She doubted she ever would again.

She returned his smile despite herself, her mouth going dry. "Promise you'll let me out when we get there."

"Of course." He seemed to study her intently, perhaps trying to figure out if she was joking. "Now hop in and I'll get you home. I imagine Mary Lapp is worried about you." He apparently knew the owner, but this shouldn't surprise her, considering they were in a small town.

As much as Hope didn't want her benefactor to worry about her, it was nice to think she might be in a situation where someone did, indeed, worry about her.

Hope slid across the vinyl back seat and was struck by how pared down the interior was. Other than seat belts, any extras had been stripped out. Probably so that prisoners didn't get any ideas. Or maybe it was easier to hose down this way. She shoved the thought aside, trying not to think about who or what had been in this back seat prior to her.

She let out a long breath, then turned her attention to the road in front of them. The deputy seemed to be checking his phone obsessively. She wondered what that was about. Her gaze shifted and she found him studying her in the rearview mirror.

"Are you new to Hunters Ridge?" he asked. "I don't recall seeing you around."

Hope's heart rate spiked far more than it should have for such a mundane question. But any personal question was a threat to her security. "Yeah." The single word came out on a squeak. "I recently took a job at the bed-and-breakfast."

"What brought you to this town? It's not exactly a thriving metropolis. I grew up here, so I came by the place honestly enough."

Hope shrugged, hating that she was trapped in this conversation. "I'm really tired, deputy," she said, suddenly feeling like a heel.

"Of course." He shifted in his seat. "Feel free to call me Travis since we're apparently neighbors."

"Neighbors?" She worried that her voice cracked.

"My land backs up to Mary's land. Once the leaves are off the trees, you can see my house. Apparently, years ago my place served as a sort of *dawdy haus* for what is now the B&B."

"Dawdy haus?"

"The Amish are a tight-knit group, if you haven't already figured that out. The grandparents usually stay right on the property of their children. In this case, they lived on the other side of the trees. Really large piece of property," he added. "Over the years, a well-worn path cut through the woods. Now it's mostly overgrown, but fun to explore. Sometimes on a Sunday morning I'll be reading the paper in my kitchen and spot some guests of Mary's B&B appear in my yard." He smiled and met her gaze in the rearview mirror. "I can always tell they're out-of-towners by the way they're dressed. Always a little too nice to be out hiking, you know."

She found herself returning his smile and nodding. She did know.

Travis laughed. "No worries, I try to mind my own business. Unless of course, it comes to my job." He adjusted the rearview mirror with one hand. "Do you have family here?"

She averted her gaze and mumbled, "No." She slumped back into her seat and pretended to take in the scenery outside the window. All she could see was her eyes, hollowed out in her pale skin, staring back at her.

His cell phone rang and he answered immediately on the Bluetooth. "Ginny?" he asked, the first sign of worry in his voice.

"Uncle Travis."

The deputy straightened in his seat and seemed to grip the steering wheel tighter. "Hey buddy, what's up?"

"I can't wake Mommy up." The scared, tiny voice floated over the line and filled the patrol car.

Travis shot her a quick glance in the rearview again, then the patrol car picked up speed, the engine roaring to life.

"It's okay, buddy. Are you at home?"

"I was camping in the tent with Cujo. I had to go pee. Mommy was sleeping on the floor." Hope's heart broke for the little boy.

"Okay, I'm five minutes away. Is there anyone else there?"

"I don't know where Daddy is."

"That's okay." Travis took a sharp left at the intersection, traveling away from the bed-and-breakfast, but Hope wasn't about to say anything. "Go into your bedroom and close the door?"

"Ok," he whispered.

"I'll tell you when it's safe to come out. I'm on my way." Travis reached over and picked up the handset to his radio. "Stay on the phone with me, buddy. I'm going to use my radio to call an ambulance. They'll help Mommy."

"Okay." The little boy sniffled, understandably not sounding too sure.

Hope's memory slammed her back to another time, a life-time ago. Her empty stomach felt queasy and a bead of sweat formed around her hairline.

Travis requested an ambulance to an address not far from the B&B.

Help's on the way. Help's on the way. Help's on the way. She tried to telegraph her words of comfort to the kid because once upon a time, she had been home alone with her mom when her mom collapsed. Back then, no one paid the phone bill, and they certainly couldn't afford cell phones. Thankfully, Miss June was home next door and called for the ambulance.

Help hadn't arrived in time.

CHAPTER 4

*T*ravis had served in the military, and he used his training to tamp down his mounting feelings of doom. *You have a job to do. Do your job. Don't make it personal.*

It is personal.

Come on, come on, come on.

He flipped the siren on and pressed the accelerator. "Buckle up," he said to his passenger in the back seat. "We have to make a detour."

In the rearview mirror he saw Hope glance down, as if to double-check her belt, but she didn't say anything.

Outside his windshield, the trees and the dark shadows of farmhouses whizzed past in the night. His palms grew sweat-slicked. His gut told him he was about to realize his worst fear regarding his older sister. His poor nephew was terrified. He had hoped to keep him on the line, but they lost the connection. Travis pressed the accelerator and the engine roared.

Come on, come on, come on.

The image of ghostly white faces staring blankly at him with foaming mouths flashed in his mind's eye. He had witnessed the tragic end of many drug addicts firsthand more times than he cared to count. Lives cut short. Families destroyed.

Addiction was a tough beast to slay, and up until a year ago he'd thought Ginny had beaten it. *Don't go there. Focus.* He huffed out a breath, hating that he had this poor woman from the laundromat in his vehicle. Her nerves must already be fried from the shock of nearly getting crushed by his irresponsible brother-in-law.

"I'm really sorry about this," Travis said, needing to focus on something other than the horrid images scrolling through his mind. "I wouldn't normally take a civilian on a call." Never mind that this was personal.

"Please don't worry about it. Do what you have to do." Obviously, she had heard the call. The pleas of his nephew. He glanced into the rearview mirror again. She had her arms wrapped around her like she was cold.

"My sister's place is right up here."

The engine purred as he climbed the familiar crest to his childhood home. His father had once owned all this land and had willed it to Ginny—and only Ginny—out of spite. The headlights swept across the farmhouse with its dingy white clapboard siding, overgrown landscaping, and a drain spout swaying in the wind, reminding him how far his sister and her husband had fallen.

He jammed the vehicle into park. "I'll be right back. Stay here." He jumped out of the vehicle and popped open the trunk to grab his Narcan kit. He hated that his gut told him he'd need it. A tapping sound drew his attention to the back window of his patrol car where Hope pounded it with her fist.

He opened her door and she practically flung herself out of the car. "I don't like feeling trapped."

Travis nodded. "Stay by the car."

"I will." The moonlight caught a flash of fear in her eyes and then it was gone. "Go!" She made a shooing gesture with her hands. "I'm sorry, I didn't mean to hold you up." Her head dipped in what seemed to be embarrassment, but he didn't have time to sort it out.

Travis gave her a quick nod, then jogged around to the back of the house, not wanting to risk falling through the decaying wood of the front porch. Last month he had picked up Aiden to go to Cub Scouts and had been shocked by the large, exposed hole on the porch—an accident waiting to happen. His sister had used it as an excuse to keep him out of the house, a place he hadn't been in since Ginny took possession years earlier.

In the backyard, Travis found a pitched tent under a starry sky. In an alternate universe, this would have been a tranquil scene. Instead an ominous dread hung over him like an oppressive blanket, making it hard to fill his lungs.

Treat it like any other call.

Travis pulled back the flap of the tent in case Aiden had retreated here. The only occupant was his nephew's faithful friend, a miniature Bernedoodle that Kerry named Cujo as a joke. A joke his son was too young to get. The furry guy was the friendliest mush ball with the name of a ferocious villain of a Stephen King novel. At some point, *Cujo*, the book, was made into a movie that Kerry had caught late one night while flipping channels, or so Ginny claimed. The man wasn't a reader, so it made sense. Travis might be inclined to say it was a funny name, but he'd never give his jerk brother-in-law the satisfaction.

Cujo lifted his head and wagged his tail, then leapt out of the tent, happy to have company. Afraid the dog might wander off, Travis led him into his four-by-six kennel at the back of the house. His brother-in-law had forced the two-year-old dog to live outside after he realized potty training wasn't as easy as it seemed.

The depth of his anger toward this man seemed bottomless. His sister claimed that Cujo was allowed in the house during the winter, but Travis wasn't sure. This was no way to treat a family pet.

Travis latched the gate on the kennel. "I'll be back soon." Cujo jumped up and rested his front paws on the chain-link fence, wagging his tail happily.

Turning his attention to the house, Travis pushed opened the back door. The smell of old garbage and burned toast lingered in the air. How could anyone live like this? "Ginny!" He called his sister's name. His heartbeat raced in his ears.

No answer.

"Aiden!" He scanned the stacks of clothing and books and video games, wondering if his young nephew was crouched down among all the detritus or if he had gone to his bedroom like he had been told. Travis stepped around a pile of black garbage bags filled with goodness knew what and found his sister sprawled on the floor, unconscious. Adrenaline surged through his veins and his mind went blank. His gaze snapped to his five-year-old nephew curled up on cracked linoleum a few feet away.

Aiden looked up with watery eyes. Dirt and tears stained his freckled cheeks. "I can't wake Mommy up."

Travis stepped over his sister and extended his hand to the little boy. The child scrambled up and lunged for him, throwing his arms around his waist and sobbing into his side.

"Come on, let's get you out of here." Travis's voice was remarkably calm despite the thrum of panic propelling him into what felt like an out-of-body experience.

This can't be happening!

Time was slipping away. He had to tend to his sister. But not with his young nephew in view.

"Mommy!" the child screamed, wildly glancing over his shoulder at his mother while Travis led him by the hand through the mess to the outside.

A mix of emotions knotted Travis's gut. This memory would be forever etched in this child's mind, much like the disastrous scenes of his own childhood that led one child to become a sheriff's deputy and the other to become...

Just like our father.

"Come on, Aiden. I've got you." Travis pushed open the door and the cool night air hit his fiery cheeks. He came up short.

Hope was crouched down in the kennel petting Cujo. She smiled at his nephew. "Is this beautiful dog yours?"

Aiden nodded, and suddenly Travis was grateful this stranger happened to be on this call with him. "Aiden, go with my friend, Ms. Baker. She'll stay with you and Cujo while I check on your mommy."

Aiden swung around and clung to Travis's waist in a death grip. He buried his face in his side. "Don't leave me!"

Hope stood and grabbed a leash dangling from the side of the kennel. "Can we take this guy for a walk? Maybe we could look for the Big Dipper." Hope's voice was like music to Travis's ears. "It's really easy to spot in the dark country sky."

Aiden eased his grip on Travis's waist and stepped away with Hope, reluctance radiating from his tiny frame.

Go, she mouthed to Travis over the boy's head.

And in that moment, a brick fell away from the wall he had built around his heart.

Who is this woman? He didn't have time to ponder that now.

"I'll be right back." Travis raced inside; the back door

slamming shut behind him. He could hear Hope's soothing voice in the yard until the walls of his childhood home closed in on him.

A bead of sweat rolled down his back. He dropped to his knees next to his sister. With tunnel vision, he checked her pulse. It was thready. He tapped her face and called her name, but she remained unresponsive. Her lips were blue. In the distance, he heard the ambulance. He snagged the Narcan kit from where he had set it when he retrieved Aiden. Thank goodness the deputies had started carrying the medication to treat a suspected opioid overdose.

He sent up a silent prayer, then administered the drug up her nose.

Ginny sat up, sucking in a huge breath, as if she had emerged after being underwater for a long time. Her eyes opened wide in shocked surprise, much like when he snuck up on her late at night and woke her from a sound sleep. He supposed a drug overdose was probably the deepest sleep a person could have.

He closed his eyes and let out a long breath between tight lips.

Ginny made abrupt, jerky movements and started to glance around. Travis placed his hand behind her head. "It's all right. You're going to be fine. Lie back."

His big sister resisted his gentle nudge, instead trying to sit up. "Where's Kerry?" she asked, her voice raspy. "You need to find Kerry."

"Relax," Travis commanded. A new surge of anger washed over him. His sister woke up from the dead and her only concern was her no-good husband? Didn't she realize her son had been here alone, terrified that his mom had died? Travis swallowed his rage like he had done as a child.

Why bother arguing? It wouldn't do any good. Ginny would have little recollection of tonight's events and would soon be out looking for whatever oblivion she had found tonight.

A commotion came from the back of the house. The paramedics pushed through the door. Their blank expressions gave no indication that they were judging the occupants for these living conditions. They had probably seen similar and worse—just as he had—in their line of work. He brought the paramedics up to date, then stepped out of the way for them to do their work.

Once Ginny was fastened to the gurney, Travis kissed the back of his sister's cool, delicate hand and placed it on her midsection. "You're going to be okay."

This time.

Ginny's head lolled to one side. "Where's Kerry? Find Kerry." Her voice was weak, and still she made no mention of her child.

Travis fisted his hand. How had that man won her devotion? Was it a case of a daughter marrying someone just like her father?

"Don't worry," Travis said, apropos of nothing. His only goal right now was to see his sister get back on her feet, and if that meant reassuring her about Kerry when it wasn't warranted, then so be it.

"Don't tell anyone," she said, barely above a whisper. She was probably afraid of losing her job. They wouldn't look kindly on drug use.

Shaking his head in frustration, Travis slipped past the two paramedics in the cramped space. Once outside, he sucked in a deep breath, the cool air filling his lungs. His sister had almost died.

Without the lifesaving medication, she would have. Dread fisted in his gut. How many times could she be found unconscious before no one was around to call for help? Before it was too late?

CHAPTER 5

*H*ope ran her hand down the child's sweaty head as he clung to her. Aiden's dog—she learned his name was Cujo—hung just as close, probably happy to be out of the kennel. She forgave the cute ball of fur for almost taking her out at the knees in his excitement. Hope had shown Aiden the Big Dipper and a few other constellations before he grew disinterested and started crying again.

"Everything will be okay." Hope felt the weight of the world in finding the right thing to say, yet she wondered if he'd even remember. Finding his mother unconscious would scar him for life. How much depended on if the woman pulled through.

Putting positive vibes out there. Please don't let her die.

"You're safe." Hope tried to reassure the little boy. Understandably, he had been reluctant to leave his uncle's side, but now he was holding on tight to her.

Her mind flashed back to her teenage years living with Miss June, her neighbor who also happened to run a foster home, when the youngest children had clung to Hope as if she was a surrogate mother. As much as she cherished giving them comfort, she was always careful to not get attached. The cute kids were always placed first. No one wanted a sullen teenager who had lost her mother to cancer on the cusp of her teenage years, leaving her with few options other than to bide her time and age out of the system. Thank goodness for Miss June.

A shudder racked down Aiden's body, snapping her out of her reverie. Hope tilted her head to try to see the boy's face, but he seemed to be fascinated with his sneakers, his toe poking out of the torn, dingy white canvas as he kicked at a patch of dirt. Cujo then pounced after the stones he freed.

"Are you cold?" Her eyes traveled to the small house with missing roof shingles and cracked windows. Tall weeds climbed up the clapboard siding, tangling the frame of an abandoned bike, a discarded BBQ pit, and various garden tools. It seemed to Hope that there had been a lot of plans for this land that had gone to die. There was no way she could bring the child back inside to warm up, and she didn't feel comfortable taking him to the patrol car. He might think he was in trouble. That was how she had felt when the CPS worker came to collect her.

She had often wondered if people blamed her for her mother's death. Shouldn't Hope have gone to Miss June when her mother started looking so tired? Instead, she had waited until it was too late. No matter how many times she had been assured her mother's cancer was terminal, Hope couldn't help but wonder if something more could have been done.

Shaking away the thought, Hope eased the boy's hand out of hers and slid off her gray hoodie. "Here, put this on. It's nice and warm." A blanket of goose bumps raced up her arms.

The cotton jacket hung down to midthigh on the child. She reached over and flipped up the hood, zipped it, and gently drew in the strings to close the gap around his exposed neck.

"How's that?"

He nodded, his eyes still downcast. She was grateful she could do this simple thing for this child, even though it had left her chilly.

"Come on," she said cheerily, taking him by the hand, acting as if they were going on some big adventure. She didn't want the boy to be standing right outside the door when the paramedics brought his mother out. The traumatized kid didn't need that in his memory bank, too.

Hope held his hand tight and walked parallel to the road, toward the neighbor's, hoping she'd be able to see when the ambulance had left. Cujo jumped and bit at the string hanging down from her jacket on the little boy. The wild weeds and overgrown grass gave way to the neighbor's well-tended yard. She didn't want to scare a homeowner by an unexpected late-night visit, so she stayed on the front lawn under a large oak tree. The homeowners must have had a penchant for gardening because there were mums clinging to their last bit of color lining a pathway to a decorative bench. Surely no one would fault her for sitting on it.

Hope patted the cool cement and her new friend joined her. Cujo obediently curled up at their feet. Their backs were to his house. Aiden pulled out a small blue stone from the pocket of her hoodie and held it up in his palm.

"I see you found my worry stone."

"Worry stone?" His little forehead bunched up.

Hope smiled and picked up the stone and rubbed it between her fingers. "You rub it like this to take away your worries." She held it out to him and he took it back.

Aiden pressed it between his fingers. "Like this?"

"Exactly." She wrapped her arms around the child, relishing in his warmth. He tucked his hand with the stone in his pocket where she imagined he was feeling the smoothness of it. After a short time, he tilted his head, rested it on her shoulder and fell asleep.

Suddenly, Hope felt very, very tired. She'd love to go to sleep herself. She closed her eyes and found herself sending all her positive energy to this child. Her mother would have told her to pray, but ever since God didn't answer her prayers to cure her mother's cancer, she'd given up on it and started sending people good thoughts. Whatever. The kid needed it, especially since his mother had overdosed in front of him, and his father had decided that driving under the influence and plowing into Wash & Go was somehow a good idea. His uncle better be a stand-up kind of guy. No one deserved to be shuffled through strangers' homes.

But sometimes the most wonderful people take a child in, she reminded herself. Like Miss June. Hope realized it could have been much worse. The kindly woman treated her like a granddaughter after her mother died. Thankfully, when Miss June's adult children convinced her that the big house was too much for her and moved her into an assisted living facility, Hope was old enough to strike out on her own. Too bad it was into the arms of Derek Wall, a police officer who seemed benevolent, until he wasn't. It took her seven years to finally get away.

A soft breeze rustled the hairs on the back of her neck and a chill raced up her spine. She cuddled Aiden closer. Had she really gotten away from Derek? Each day she lived with the fear of his sudden return. She'd never be free.

"Hope." Travis called her name, and his deep voice did something unexpected to her insides.

She shifted as best she could while holding the boy on the cold cement bench. The dog remained content at their feet.

"I saw you crossing the yard," the deputy said, as if explaining how he had found her. "Thank you for looking out for my nephew." He kept his voice low and the child showed no signs of waking up.

"How is she?" Hope whispered.

"Alive." The single word was fraught with emotion. The moonlight glistened in his eyes and for the first time since she had snuck out on Derek with only a few possessions and the clothes on her back, she thought about what it would be like to be with a man who truly cared.

You thought Derek cared at first. You were wrong.

"Aiden has been a trouper, but he's exhausted," she said, needing to focus on something concrete, and not the distracted thoughts of a life she'd probably never have.

"Poor kid." Travis reached out and gently touched his nephew's cheek with his knuckles. "The ambulance took my sister to the hospital. I can take you home now."

Hope wanted to stay, to comfort this child, but she knew it wasn't her place. He was a stranger to her. They both were. "Thanks," she said simply. "I'd appreciate that."

Travis scooped up his nephew, who looked puny in his strong arms. The child's head lolled against his uncle's broad shoulder. They both had the same color hair, brown with flecks of gold that glistened in the moonlight. She wondered if in twenty-five years, Aiden would have the same midnight shadow on his square jaw.

Hope stood and swiped at her backside. Embarrassment heated her cheeks. Maybe she should have gone to the hospital to get checked out. Maybe she had whacked her head and didn't remember, because she couldn't figure out why she found herself attracted to this man, when a man was the last thing she needed in her life.

Travis carried his nephew across the yard. Hope grabbed Cujo's leash as he followed his human, his fluffy tail wagging. This time, Hope didn't mind sitting in the back seat. It allowed her to comfort the child. After making sure they were both buckled, she adjusted his head so that he was leaning comfortably against her shoulder while the dog sniffed her hair, then checked out the floorboards before nudging Aiden's thigh. Hope scratched the dog's head and smiled. "You're such a good boy, aren't you?" A person couldn't remain in the dumps with a cute little dog like Cujo around.

"Mary Lapp's B&B?" Travis asked, looking into the rearview mirror for confirmation, and she nodded. It seemed like a long time ago that he had set off to take her home, only to be sidetracked to his sister's house.

Aiden's even breathing and the occasional chirp of the police radio broke the companionable silence. Once in the driveway of the bed-and-breakfast, she unbuckled. "Ugh, I hate to leave him. He's sleeping so well." Cujo was curled in a ball on the back seat. He lifted his head, then set it back down on the boy's leg.

"I think he'll sleep well no matter what." The deputy opened his door. "Hold up while I grab something." He went into the trunk, then opened the back door and tucked a folded sweatshirt under his nephew's head. With Hope's help, he shifted his nephew so that his head was resting on the fabric, the seat belt stretched across him. "Thanks."

They locked gazes and Hope was the first to look away. She had to get out of here. She reached for the opposite door handle and found it locked. She glanced back, heat warming her cheeks. "I guess you wouldn't want your prisoners to escape."

Through the open door, he offered his hand. He had a solid grip, but he didn't squeeze her knuckles like her ex often did. One of his power plays. She carefully slid around Aiden who was now stretched across the back seat. Once on her feet, she dropped Travis's hand and took a step back, creating distance between them. Travis shut the door and Cujo, suddenly worried he was going to be left behind, hopped up and rested his paws on the edge of the window. Condensation formed on the glass where his little nose pressed.

"He is such a cute dog," Hope said, finding herself smiling again. "I always wanted a dog, but…" She lifted her gaze to Travis's and found him studying her. What was she going on about? She shook her head, dismissing the thought. "Well, thanks for the ride."

"Any time," he said, his voice deep and welcoming.

Hope strode to the door. She could feel Travis's eyes on her. She sensed he would have escorted her to the door if it hadn't been for his nephew. She found herself wondering what it would be like if they had met at another time and place, and he had been bringing her home from a date. Would he have kissed her at the door?

Hope pressed the heel of her hand to her forehead. *Stop*—the poor man was stressed about his sister and she was thinking about dating him? *Ugh.*

Hope twisted the door handle and Mary met her just inside, her eyes filled with worry.

"I'm so glad you're home." The older woman stood at the open door and watched the patrol car pull away. "A sheriff's deputy dropped you off? That was nice."

"I'm fine," Hope reassured her. "And I'm really sorry about your van."

"Thank *Gott* you're okay." The woman reached out as if to pull her into a hug, then seemed to check herself and dropped her arms to her side, then crossed them over her chest.

Hope had never known her to be affectionate, even with Ada. She assumed perhaps it was an Amish thing.

"That's all that matters," Mary added. "Material things can be replaced."

Hope patted the back pocket of her jeans absentmindedly. "I have the business card from the garage. Oh…" Her heart sank. "I'm afraid I left the tablecloths at the laundromat." She realized none of this was her fault, but she had spent a significant part of her life since her mother's death learning to be compliant and conflict adverse. Making sure she wasn't any trouble to Miss June. And then Derek.

"Dear, none of that is important. What can I get you? Are you hurt at all?" The tenderness in Mary's voice brought Hope to the brink of breaking down.

Hope bit back the emotion, afraid if she let the tears fall, she'd never regain her composure. "I'm a little shaken up. That's all." She hadn't even shared the bit about going to the house where a child's mother overdosed. It was all too much. Too much. "I'm going to go to bed. I'm tired."

"Of course you are." Mary clasped her hands in front of her in a gesture that reminded Hope of her mother.

"Good night," Hope said as she turned toward the stairs.

"Guten nacht."

Hope climbed the stairs and found Ada, Mrs. Lapp's teenage daughter, on the landing. "What happened?" The teen's eyes shone bright in the moonlight streaming through the window.

"Someone drove through the front of the laundromat."

"Really? Wow. Were they drinking or something?"

"Something." That was for the sheriff's department to sort out.

"The van's gone?" Ada spoke in hushed whispers.

"For now." Hope narrowed her gaze at the girl curiously.

"Oh." The girl seemed dejected.

Hope kept her mouth closed, waiting for the young Amish girl to reveal her secret because Hope could tell she had one.

"I wonder if my *mem* will replace it." There was a faraway quality to the girl's voice.

"What's going on, Ada?" Hope asked, rubbing her eyes. She could feel the beginning of a migraine aura zigging and zagging in her line of vision. *Yech.*

The girl glanced downstairs, apparently making sure her mother wasn't within earshot, then leaned in closer. "Little Amos is supposed to teach me how to drive."

"I'm sure it'll be fixed soon," Hope said, not wanting to get into whether she thought it was a good idea for a nice Amish girl to learn how to drive against the rules of the church. "Your mom needs a van to run the B&B."

"I hope so," Ada said and spun around, her white sleeping gown hanging down past her knees. She closed the door to her bedroom.

Hope might have felt slighted that the girl was selfishly only concerned with her own interests, but really, all of this was none of her business. Yet despite her best efforts to stick to herself, earn some money, and figure out her next steps, Hope Baker, formerly known as Harper Miller, seemed to find herself in the thick of it.

CHAPTER 6

*W*hen Travis dropped Hope off at the B&B, he was relieved to see someone had waited up for her. He felt funny about not walking her to the door, and splitting after everything she had been through tonight, but it wasn't his place. He had just met the woman, yet something about the way she'd tended to his nephew touched his heart.

Who is this Hope Baker? The question occupied his mind, even as his sister's health weighed on him. And his sweet little nephew dozing in the back seat would wake up to find neither of his parents there. He cursed them under his breath.

Hope was a bright light in an otherwise miserable evening. She seemed reserved, but that made her more intriguing. Why was she working at an Amish bed-and-breakfast? Why was she in Hunters Ridge? She had seemed hesitant to give him her name at the accident site, which was the first thing that piqued his interest. Maybe she was lying.

Travis slowed at an intersection and looked both ways before proceeding. He had seen far too many horrific accidents. His mind drifted again. Everything about Hope screamed *Englisch*, from her jeans to the way she talked. He didn't detect the familiar Pennsylvania Dutch lilt. She definitely wasn't former Amish. Did she have Amish roots?

Maybe he was reading too much into this. The young woman had barely escaped with her life when his idiot brother-in-law plowed into the storefront.

Maybe she was just trying to live her life in peace without him studying her. Her initial aloofness was probably from nerves. And she seemed to be more herself when she was comforting his nephew. He was grateful for that. His poor nephew. Travis would have to make sure Hope knew he appreciated everything she had done for him and his family tonight. Maybe he could thank her with flowers or dinner. He smiled to himself in the darkened cab of his patrol car. Maybe he was being selfish because he wanted to see her again.

"Is Mommy dead?" Aiden asked from the back seat, jolting Travis out of his thoughts. He wished he wasn't driving so he could look the boy in the eyes to reassure him.

"No, no, buddy. Your mom went to the hospital. The doctors will take good care of her." Travis didn't want to offer any promises he couldn't keep, but in his heart he believed his tough older sister would be okay. She always had been. Travis looked up but couldn't find Aiden's face in the rearview mirror. "You doing okay back there?"

"Yeah," the kid muttered. "Cujo wants to go home."

"Soon," Travis said noncommittally. "How about you guys stay at my place tonight? We'll have a sleepover."

Travis could imagine the little kid shrugging his shoulders.

"Have you ever ridden in a sheriff's vehicle before tonight?" Travis asked, trying to distract the kid.

"No, but my dad has. Mom called 911 and they took him

away even though she changed her mind." There was a hard edge to the boy's voice. "My dad said people need to mind their business."

A queasy feeling settled in his gut. *Great. Just great.* Travis hadn't been at work when that happened a couple weeks ago, but word got around.

"My job is to make sure people are safe. I'm sure if the deputy made your dad go with him, it was for a good reason."

A heavy silence filled the space. He'd need to cut the kid some slack after everything he had been through. You couldn't expect a child of someone who disrespected law enforcement to suddenly admire them.

"Was your dad at the house tonight?" Travis asked. "Before your mom got sick?"

"They were fighting. Mom told him to go to—" Aiden stopped abruptly. "I'm not supposed to say that word. It's a bad word."

"It's okay, little man. I get the idea." The irony that his sister was cursing out her husband while also raising her child not to say "bad words" wasn't lost on him.

"Can't I stay with Dad while Mommy is sick?"

Travis carefully measured his words because he couldn't tell the kid his dad was also in the hospital, probably cuffed to the bed rails. "Tonight you'll stay with me."

Aiden let out a long-suffering sigh, sounding like someone much older.

"Hey." Travis tried to sound cheery. "You think Cujo would make a good K-9 officer?"

"Aren't K-9s supposed to be German shepherds?"

"Mostly, yeah. But it'd be fun to train Cujo to do some drills, wouldn't it? Maybe we could do that." Travis was searching for a distraction.

"Maybe," Aiden finally said. "I'll ask my mom."

Travis slowed as he pulled into his driveway. They didn't

have far to go from the B&B. "Sounds like a plan." He prayed the child's mom would be around to ask.

The next morning, Travis called the hospital to get an update on his sister. Due to privacy laws, he couldn't get much information, but at least no one had tracked him down in the past twelve hours to tell him his sister was dead.

He hung up the phone and decided he'd have to go in person to check on her. He turned and found Aiden standing in the doorway staring at him, Cujo panting at his side. His nephew had on the same clothes from last night and Travis wished he had thought to pack a bag for him. Then, remembering how his sister's house could be a finalist for the show *Hoarders*, he figured he probably would have had a hard time finding something clean. Perhaps they could run to the superstore the next town over to pick up some things. He'd need pet supplies, too.

But first things first.

"You hungry?" Travis found a solitary box of Cheerios in the cabinet. He unrolled the bag and tasted a few O's. Not too bad. His breakfast usually consisted of coffee with two creams and two sugars, so the only reason he had a box of cereal was for the times Aiden came over. Unfortunately, the last couple months that hadn't been too often other than to pick the kid up for Scouts. Ginny was probably trying to hide her relapse. Mentally he cursed himself for not being more on top of things.

Guilt is a horrible master.

Shaking aside his thoughts, he opened the fridge and frowned. Well, he had cereal, but he lacked the requisite milk. No kid liked to eat dry cereal unless it was in the same category as Froot Loops. He closed the fridge and turned to Aiden. "Maybe we could go out to eat?"

Aiden shrugged, and something about the gesture—his mannerisms—reminded Travis of his sister. His nephew pulled out a stool and plunked down, resting his elbows on the table. "My belly hurts."

Travis looked around. "Some toast, maybe?"

The kid shrugged again. Travis's dinners were usually cold-cut sandwiches or soup, so he had bread, thankfully. He made some toast and slid it in front of his nephew with a glass of water. Aiden's father was probably getting a better meal in custody this morning. Travis had gotten word that the sheriff's department had transported him from the hospital to lockup sometime overnight. It amazed Travis that his brother-in-law hadn't been more seriously hurt in the accident.

Travis made his coffee, then fed Cujo a few bits of toast. The dog was more excited about his breakfast than his big brother. "Are you thirsty?" Travis talked in that high-pitched voice that dog lovers use. Cujo cocked his head in rapt attention, making Travis believe he'd respond in words if he could. "I'll get you some water. Would you like that? Yeah, I know you'd like that." He filled a glass bowl and set it on the floor. The dog lapped it up greedily. They would have to figure things out if these two were going to be staying with him indefinitely.

Travis splashed some half-and-half in his coffee, then added the sugar. He sat down on the stool next to his nephew and was about to offer him something else to eat when his phone on the table next to him rang. The special ringtone he had set for his mother made his stomach clench. Someone had told her about Ginny. And it hadn't been him. Word traveled fast in a small town. He'd pay for that transgression. His mother, the paranoid type, already complained that her only surviving family was conspiring against her. She never seemed to consider their strained relationship was because she'd chosen drugs over her children for most of their lives. Just because she was currently sober didn't give her a pass.

He stared at the phone for a hot minute, debating if he should answer it. Ignoring her call right now would be cruel.

Travis was many things, but cruel wasn't one of them.

"Hello," he said, swinging around on the stool so that his back was to his nephew.

"How come I had to hear about your sister from Sandy?"

"Sandy?" Travis repeated, trying to place the name.

"Yeah, Sandy. Peg's daughter. She's a nurse in the ER."

I suppose Sandy isn't worried about a HIPAA violation. He kept that thought to himself.

"I wanted to check on Ginny this morning before I called," he fibbed. He would have told her eventually, but probably not this morning. Not with Aiden in his care. "I didn't want you to worry." He kept his voice low, but he figured Aiden was listening intently to everything he said.

"Virginia hasn't been eating enough. She's malnourished." Their mother hated her daughter's nickname and refused to call her Ginny.

Ah, that might explain why she hasn't been discharged. Travis had heard of some overdose victims being released from the ER without being admitted after they'd stabilized.

Travis stepped into the other room. "Mom, you know what happened, right? Sandy told you the whole story?"

"She did." His mother's words came out clipped. "Your sister needs more willpower. The whole town will be talking."

Travis wondered if his mother would have more sympathy if she herself hadn't been a recovered addict. His parents divorced after she cleaned up her life, but despite this, she remained at arm's length with her children. A person couldn't do what she did to her children while they were growing up and expect all to be forgiven.

"I'll do what I can to get her into treatment," Travis said, wondering how receptive Ginny would be. As far as he knew, she had been two years clean before this recent overdose.

"Now where is my grandson?"

Travis peeked into the kitchen. Aiden had eaten one piece of toast and was working on the second unenthusiastically. Well, he thought that was the case until he realized the boy was stretching his hand down to his dog, feeding him bits of toast.

"That boy needs structure in his life," his mother yapped in his ear, "and goodness knows that idiot of a father isn't going to provide it. And your sister is far too soft. She always has been."

Travis turned his back to his nephew and walked deeper into the dining room, anger burning his ears. His mother was brutally critical without much self-awareness. But arguing with her would only escalate her indignation. "I've got him. He's fine," Travis said.

"Don't be silly," his mother said. "You have to work. He can come stay with me." His mother lived in a retirement community not far from Hunters Ridge. Travis imagined Aiden sitting in her small apartment that was too warm twelve months of the year, being told to hush because he might disturb the downstairs neighbors.

"Mother," he said more forcefully, "Aiden can stay here with me." He hadn't figured out the details, but he'd make it happen. He hoped.

"Put him on the phone."

"No, Mother."

"Aiden! Aiden!" his mother shouted.

Travis put the phone on mute and anger pulsed through

his veins. He stepped into the kitchen. "Your grandmother is on the phone. Do you want to talk to her?"

That shrug again.

"Is it okay if I put her on speakerphone? I'll be right here."

"Okay," Aiden finally said.

"Mother," Travis said, getting her attention, "I have you on speaker. Aiden's here."

"I hate being put on blast. You know that." This from the woman who had only moments ago been screaming her grandson's name in his ear.

Say hello, he mouthed to Aiden.

"Hi," he said half-heartedly, and Travis braced himself. Agreeing to this conversation was a bad idea for an already frail child. But per usual, despite dealing with drunks, thieves and all-around bad guys, Travis couldn't manage his own mother.

"Now dear, speak up so I can hear you," his mother said, true to form.

"Hi," Aiden shouted and Travis had to turn his face away when he laughed.

"Your Uncle Travis is going to drop you off over here."

Aiden's eyebrows shot up, then his face went white before he started crying. Silent tears streaked down his face while he pressed his trembling lips together. Travis placed his hand on the boy's shoulder. Cujo nudged the side of Aiden's thigh, trying to cheer him up. What a good boy. "You don't have to go."

"Hush, Travis. Of course he wants to come here. You're making way too much out of this. It's the obvious solution. It's been far too long since I've seen my only grandchild."

Travis did have a job, and Aiden was too young to stay by himself.

Maybe just temporarily, Travis rationalized. Maybe he was being stubborn.

Until…until what? His sister got out of the hospital to overdose again? Till Aiden's father straightened up, if ever?

"I can take a few vacation days until we figure this out."

"Don't be silly," his mother said, as if he had personally offended her. Perhaps he had. Everything was personal to his mother.

"The dog would be coming with him," Travis said, convinced that would be the final straw.

"That's fine," his mother said when Travis suspected it wasn't really.

"If you're sure, we'll be by later today." Travis ended the call even as his mother protested. He slid onto the stool next to his nephew. "Will you be okay at Grandma's for a few days?" Even though Travis was the adult, the one who would make the final decision, he wanted the poor kid's buy-in. Aiden had already been through so much.

"Mommy says Grandma is evil."

Aiden's even tone sent a jolt to Travis's heart. Ginny and his mother never got along. They were too much alike. His mother, no doubt, saw Ginny as her biggest failure. In return, Ginny blamed her mother for her addictive personality. Whenever the two were in the same room, it was like a bomb waiting to go off.

"She's not all that bad, is she?" Travis felt like a bit of a hypocrite. He rarely visited his mother, and now he was trying to convince his nephew that it was a perfectly good place to stay until his parents could care for him again. Or at least until Travis could come up with another plan.

Aiden sniffed. "Cujo can come?" His tone held a hint of compromise.

"Absolutely. I'll make you a deal." Travis pulled his wallet out of his back pocket and grabbed a business card. "My cell phone number is here. You can read numbers, right?"

The little boy nodded.

"Call me if you need anything and I'll come get you."

"Promise." Aiden looked up, his eyes wide with hope, looking for confirmation that one adult in his life wasn't going to let him down.

"I promise." A nagging tugged at him. He feared this promise would be tough to keep because he was in no position to care for a child, but goodness knew, neither were Aiden's parents. Not now, anyway.

Aiden rubbed his eyes. "I don't have my stuff. It's at home."

"Do you know how to write a list?" Travis asked.

Aiden straightened and a proud smile brightened his face. "Some words. Mom taught me."

"Okay, great." Travis could imagine his sister—healthy and clear-eyed—taking a keen focus on her son's education. She had always been the smart one. She had big plans for college until she met Kerry and all her plans for the future got derailed.

Travis grabbed a pen and piece of paper and patted the table in front of Aiden. "Make a list of everything you need from your house. I'll get it later. And maybe I can grab some new things from the store."

Aiden took the pen and carefully wrote his name at the top of the paper. He wrote *blanket* and *shoe*, then looked up and said, "I want my blue sneakers but I can't remember how to spell sneakers."

Travis slid into the chair next to him. "You've got a great start. Would you like to tell me what else you need and I'll write it down?"

Aiden nodded and handed his uncle the pen. "Sometimes I don't write so good."

"You've done a great job. What else do you need?" His nephew rattled off a few items and Travis wrote them down. "Sounds like you thought of everything."

Aiden's lips twitched, as if suddenly realizing what this meant. "Why can't I go home?"

"This is only temporary. Your mom needs to get better."

"Where's my dad?" Aiden asked, his nostrils trembling.

Aw man, why did this have to be so hard? He kissed the top of Aiden's head. "I'm going to check on your mom and dad. And in the meantime, if you need anything, I promise I'll be there for you." He slid the note and pen back in front of his nephew.

"Okay." The corners of Aiden's lips turned down.

Travis cleaned up the kitchen dishes, then went to the door to grab his nephew's shoes. A gray jacket sat in a pool on the floor. He picked it up and a smooth blue stone fell out of the pocket. He carried them into the kitchen. "Whose jacket is this?" A hint of fragrance reached his nose and something stirred in his belly. "Hope, from last night?"

Aiden nodded, distracted by whatever he was writing. "Yep."

Travis folded the jacket and placed it on the counter. "I suppose I'll have to return this later." Suddenly, he was looking forward to later.

His nephew looked up for the first time from his note. "Can I go with you?"

Travis tilted his head, surprised. It was the first upbeat moment from his nephew since Travis had found him traumatized by Ginny's overdose. "Sure, if that's what you'd like."

CHAPTER 7

*I*t was so, so hot. Hope was burning up. She felt the wall until she came to the door. She twisted the knob. It was locked. Panicked, she spun around. She opened her eyes wide but couldn't see. It was pitch-black.

"I'll let you out when you stop acting a fool." Derek. He always got this way when he was drunk. Suspicious. Angry. Possessive.

Let me out! Let me out! Let me out! *The words were trapped in her throat. Her lips felt like they were glued together. The walls were closing in on her.*

They had gone to the bar after a baseball game. The department had a team. One of his fellow officers said hello to her. Asked her where she was from. Was Hope supposed to be rude to his friends? How was she supposed to keep track of all the rules? On another day, Derek might have punished her for ignoring his superior or co-worker. Embarrassing him. But now she was being too friendly. She couldn't win.

She grabbed the door handle again. This time it fell off in her hands. She started sobbing. Please, please, please, she wanted to cry, but her voice was still mute.

Hope wasn't going to put up with this. Not anymore. She'd

leave him. She had nowhere to go. She'd figure something out. She couldn't live like this.

Suddenly, as if by magic, Derek's breath heated the back of her sweaty neck. "You're not going anywhere."

How had he gotten inside the locked room? How had he read her mind?

"You're mine." He twisted his fist around her hair and tugged.

Hope jerked awake. Another nightmare. Was it really a surprise after the night she'd had? Her T-shirt was sticking to her damp skin. She tossed back the quilt and climbed out of bed. Slowing her breathing to calm her nerves, she opened the window a crack to let in fresh air and the sound of crickets.

I'm safe. I'm safe.

Up bright and early after her restless sleep, Hope swept the hardwood floors, grateful to have something to occupy her time and her mind. Until she had immersed herself in the technology-free lifestyle that was normal for the Amish, she hadn't realized how cluttered her mind had become. Constantly checking the news or social media sites was addicting and often affected her mood. She'd get a jab of jealousy when a friend posted about their wedding, or their awesome vacation, or even just their quiet evening at home with their "soul mate." Of course, they could have been full of it, projecting something that didn't exist. She had been guilty of crafting idyllic posts of her magical life with Derek that didn't exist. It shamed her to think of her deceit.

Footsteps sounded on the stairs and Hope set the broom aside. *The newlyweds.* Sawyer had a duffel bag strap over his shoulder, and with his free hand he guided his new wife, Tessa, down the stairs.

"Can I help you with anything?"

Tessa held her palm to her baby bump and smiled. Her cheeks were rosy and she seemed genuinely happy. There was no faking that. "No, thank you. Breakfast was wonderful. Now we're going to get out of your hair."

"No hurry. We're not expecting more guests until next weekend," Hope said, unable to peel her eyes from the couple. If they weren't looking into each other's eyes, they were touching hands, or he had his hand on her back. They were truly in love and she wished them only happiness, especially after everything they had been through.

"Yes, great breakfast and wonderful accommodations," Sawyer said.

"I'll be sure to let Mary know. Thank you." Hope hustled ahead of them and opened the door. "Where to now?" She couldn't imagine they were headed home already. They had only gotten married yesterday. Since they had agreed to a simple wedding, Sawyer surprised his new bride with a baby shower last night. Hope smiled to herself. Where could she find a guy like this?

"We're going to Niagara Falls for a night or two," he said.

"Not too far in case this kiddo decides to come early," Tessa added, beaming up at her new husband, then turning her attention to Hope. "Have you ever been to the falls?"

"Hasn't everyone who lives in Western New York?" Hope forced a laugh, careful not to reveal anything personal about her life. Anyone who had grown up in Buffalo had taken every out-of-town visitor to Niagara Falls. Not that Hope had a lot of visitors, but Miss June made sure they did some fun things on her limited budget.

Both Sawyer and Tessa politely laughed as they headed out.

Hope lifted her hand and waved. "Have a great trip and best of luck with the little one."

"Thank you," they said in unison.

Hope stood in the doorway, enjoying the fresh air. She watched Sawyer help Tessa into the vehicle. They left and headed east toward Niagara Falls. She went back inside and picked up the broom again. When she was done here, she'd go upstairs and clean the guest room.

Her mind drifted and she wondered if Tessa or Sawyer was the type to post wedding or vacation photos to their social media timelines. Something told her they weren't. Although they seemed friendly enough, they struck her as private kind of people. Hope did, however, make a mental note to be careful not to get caught in the background of a guest's photo which could end up plastered on the internet. It wouldn't take a super sleuth to track her down from there.

Hope had grown to enjoy her anonymity in Hunters Ridge, but every so often she had been tempted to go to the library, sign on to one of the public computers, and log onto her social media sites. Not to post, of course, but to read up on what people had been saying about her. She had been gone for a month. People had to have their theories on where she disappeared to. Maybe Derek had the nerve to make a tearful plea for her return. But ultimately, fear kept her away.

She wasn't a Luddite, but she didn't know the full capabilities law enforcement had to track someone down. Perhaps they could see she had checked her social media accounts, which might lead them to the IP address in the library in Hunters Ridge. She couldn't take that chance.

After more time passed, the urge eased, and so did her mind. The Amish were on to something. This whole disconnecting thing. It was a peaceful way of life, not concerning herself with travel photos from a vacation she'd never be able to afford or wondering what secrets lurked beneath their smiling faces. Sad that she had become so jaded.

However, on a day like today she might enjoy her earbuds

and some music to drown out the replay in her mind of the explosion of glass raining down over the laundromat, coupled with the scared eyes of that little boy. That sweet little boy.

"Hope?"

She stopped sweeping and turned to find Ada standing in the doorway in a black dress with matching bonnet.

"Penny for your thoughts?" Mary's daughter arched a brow.

"Just tired after everything last night," Hope said.

Ada took the broom from her and placed it against the wall. "Today is a day of rest. Mem and I are headed to church service at the Troyers'. Would you like to come?"

Hope wasn't much of a churchgoer. She glanced down at her T-shirt and jeans. "I might stick out a bit."

"I bet one of my plain dresses would fit." Ada tipped her head toward the door, obviously enthused about the idea.

"Leave her be," Mary said, appearing in the doorway. By nature, the Amish were not looking to recruit members. "Ada is right, however. Today is a day of rest. Chores can keep."

"Yes, of course." Hope couldn't help but feel like she had been scolded.

"Did our guests get off okay?" Mary's gaze drifted to the kitchen window that overlooked the yard.

"Yes. They're headed to Niagara Falls now."

"I heard." Mary pressed her lips together. "I hope they don't wander too far. That baby is coming soon."

"There are plenty of hospitals in Buffalo," Hope said.

"I suppose so," Mary replied.

Hope watched Mary and Ada head out the door for church. It didn't start for another hour, but they'd have to hitch the horse to the buggy. One of these Sundays, she might attend out of curiosity. The Amish held services in each other's homes, every other week. Even though her mother had taken her to a nondenominational church while she was growing up, her attendance stopped altogether after her mother's death. Even when her mother was alive, Sunday was just another day filled with a multitude of activities with church squeezed in. Her mother was an incredibly hard worker and seemed to lack the "sit down and watch TV" gene. Until she became sick. Then she'd struggled to do anything.

Hope grabbed her book and settled into a rocking chair in the sitting room with her feet propped on the hearth. She looked forward to when it became cold enough to light a fire in the fireplace. Would she still be here?

The sound of gravel under tires pulled her out of her story and sent gooseflesh racing across her skin. She set her book down on the brick hearth and peered out the window. A sheriff's SUV was pulling up the driveway. Her heart kicked up a beat when she recognized Deputy Travis Hart climbing out of the vehicle. Had he tried to look up her fake name in the system and couldn't find her? Did he have follow-up questions? Trying to quell her rioting thoughts, she squared her shoulders. *Don't go down a dark tunnel. Go to the door. See what he wants.*

I did nothing wrong.

She drew in a deep breath, opened the door, and found herself facing that darn handsome smile again. She had gotten good at pretending, but something in this man's eyes suggested he didn't miss much.

"Deputy Hart," Hope said breezily. "Is there something I can do for you?"

He lifted his hand with a familiar piece of gray fabric. "Here's your sweatshirt."

Hope released an audible whoosh of breath. *He's returning my hoodie. That's all.* "Oh, thank you."

The deputy tilted his head with a curious expression on his face. "Were you expecting something else?"

Hope ran her hand across the back of her neck, feeling a layer of sweat. "I…um…" she stammered. "When I saw the sheriff's patrol vehicle, I got nervous." She hiked her chin toward his casual clothes. The blue of his college sweatshirt was a good color on him. "But you're off duty."

"Yeah, sometimes I take a vehicle home in case I get called in." He shrugged and something about his "aw shucks" demeanor made her think of Aiden. "Didn't mean to make you concerned. Sorry about that."

"No worries. How is your sister? And Aiden?" She accepted the jacket and something fell and hit the grass, distracting them both.

Travis reached over, picked it up and presented her favorite worry stone to her in his open palm. "Aiden wants to know where he can get one of these for himself. He likes the way it feels."

She plucked the blue stone from his hand and smiled at the memory of his young nephew running his little fingers over it, asking her a bunch of questions. "Please, let him keep it."

The deputy palmed the stone. "Thank you. That's nice of you." He turned and she followed his gaze. A little face popped up over the dash.

"Oh, Aiden's with you. Is he okay?"

Travis scrubbed his hand over his head. "Poor kid. He's quiet." He seemed to be holding back. "The hospital says my sister's stable, but she has a lot of other health issues due to her drug use." The anguish in his eyes softened the hard edges of concern. "I'm making some calls to try to get her into rehab."

"You're a good brother." Hope wanted to reassure him

that everything would be okay, but she didn't know that. Neither of them did.

"I don't feel like I've been a good brother." Something flashed in the depths of his eyes. Shame? Embarrassment? Something altogether different? She didn't know him well enough to decipher the exact emotion.

"Is Aiden going to stay with you for a bit?" she asked as the silence stretched a beat too long.

"My mother offered to take him. She lives in an apartment not too far away." Hope wondered if he realized he winced when he said that.

"You're not happy about that?"

"My mother isn't exactly the grandmotherly type." He lifted his hand. "I shouldn't criticize. She is stepping up to help, after all. I have a job, and he's too young to stay home alone." He crossed his arms and rolled back on his heels.

Hope had been too stressed to notice how truly handsome he was. Well, maybe that was a lie. She had, but her nerves were too jacked on adrenaline to appreciate his looks as much as she did now.

"If you need help…" Hope wasn't sure why she offered. The last thing she wanted was to get involved with someone from law enforcement. Been there, done that. This man needed to go away.

"Thanks," he said, seemingly surprised. "I'll keep that in mind."

Hope glanced toward the house. "I better get back to work." She wasn't sure why she said that, perhaps because telling him she needed to get back to her novel seemed rude. Work couldn't wait, a book could.

"Sure thing."

Hope watched him walk back to his vehicle. She waved to Aiden. The little boy waved back and a flood of affection warmed her heart. She turned around and stepped inside.

When she was about to close the door, she saw Aiden running toward her. Cujo was right on his heels.

Aiden held out his hand with the worry stone in it. "Thank you so much, Miss Hope. I won't lose it, I promise."

Something in her heart melted. "You're very welcome. Now make sure when worries get you down to rub, rub, rub them away."

"I will." That was the most energetic she had seen the little boy.

"Oh, and keep it away from Cujo, okay?" Hope held out her hand, allowing the dog to sniff it.

Aiden nodded with wide eyes, then spun around and ran back to the truck where Travis was holding the back door open for him. Cujo obediently followed, apparently unwilling to miss his chance to go for another car ride. Hope waved, then quickly ducked inside. Nostalgic and sad for something she'd never be able to have.

For the past year, she had focused solely on escaping her abusive boyfriend. Now that she had done that—*please, please, please let him never find me*—she realized she had nothing new to look forward to. She was spending each day in the moment. Survival mode.

When—if ever—would she allow herself to carve out a brighter future? She feared she was too damaged to find happiness again.

CHAPTER 8

*A*fter swinging by the B&B, Travis's next stop was his sister's house. He had long ago ceased calling it his childhood home, even though it was where he had spent his formative years. He had zero attachment to it. He wondered if he could pinpoint when he had flipped that switch in his mind. Was it after his parents divorced and his miserable father lived here alone, spewing out his hateful comments? He definitely didn't consider this place home then. Or was it after the old man died and willed the property to his sister? At that point, it was no longer his house legally. But the true break probably came when his sister and her husband started to slide down the same slippery slope as his parents. It hurt Travis that he couldn't do anything about it, despite his job enforcing the laws.

I should have been able to do something!

Now his only reason for staying connected—coming back to this place that held so many dark memories—was for the little boy in the back seat.

"You and Cujo wait here," Travis said, glancing over his shoulder. "I'll be right back."

"I want to come, too." Aiden released his seat belt and leaned forward, making Travis think he had better get a booster seat for his nephew if he was going to be driving him around on a regular basis.

Travis held up the piece of paper. "I've got your list. Why don't we treat this as a game and see how many things I can get right? You get a dollar for every item I forget." When his nephew didn't answer right away, Travis added, "Okay?"

His nephew sighed and leaned back. "Okay." It wasn't exactly the enthusiastic response he had been hoping for.

Travis hopped out of the SUV and ran around back. He could hear Cujo barking, hopping from window to window. Travis had the key to the back door of the house, something he'd had in his possession since he had lived there. This was the first time he had used it. He opened the door and the pungent smell hit home. How did his sister and her family live like this? Dirty, crusted dishes sat on top of dirty, crusted dishes. He flipped the faucet only to confirm what he suspected. No water.

He became disgusted all over again while pushing through the piles of junk lining the floors and walls to get to his nephew's bedroom, the same bedroom he had slept in as a kid. Aiden kept his room clean, probably the only thing he could control. Travis easily found his favorite pair of PJ's, the book he requested, and a few Pokémon figurines on his desk. Travis grabbed some more clean clothes and made his way back out of the house.

Travis struggled to imagine what Aiden had seen in his short life. It was unlikely the child would ever forget his mother's near-death in front of him. Would he ever be able to go back to living in this house without being haunted by that night?

This place should be condemned.

Travis gulped in the crisp fall air as soon as he stepped

outside the house. He plastered on a smile as he strode to the patrol vehicle. He handed Aiden the Pokémon guys. "I think I got everything." Cujo jumped up on the seat and sniffed all the items.

"Thanks, Uncle Travis," Aiden said quietly.

He was such a good kid that it broke Travis's heart. No kid should have to go through what he'd gone through. And he was only five years old.

"Let's go get what we need at the store," Travis said, pressing the ignition button. He'd buy this kid the biggest, most expensive Lego set if it put a smile on his face. Travis needed to do something to get rid of this gnawing sense of guilt that he could have done more for his sister and her little boy.

"I think Cujo missed you," Travis said after they got back into the vehicle after their trip through the superstore. He looked up into the rearview mirror and watched as Aiden scrunched up his face as the dog excitedly licked him. "I told you he'd be okay with the windows cracked. We weren't long."

Thankfully, knowing the dog was waiting for them hurried his nephew, who often took forever when picking out new toys.

"You ready to go see Grandma?" Travis asked after they both buckled in. Cujo rested his snout on Aiden's lap in the back seat.

His nephew sighed heavily, seemingly having the weight of the world on his shoulders. It was a marked transformation from the little boy who had just picked up a police station Lego set and got puppy kisses.

"Can I stay with you instead?" Aiden asked.

"You have my phone number. Call me and I'll get you

anytime." Travis hoped it didn't come to that. His mother would have a meltdown if he took away her grandson just when he was finally within her grasp again. Ginny and her mother's crummy relationship had damaged her relationship with her grandson. It took his sister's near-death for their mother to get to see Aiden again. A pang of guilt hit Travis. His sister would probably never forgive him for this betrayal.

But what choice did he have? He had to work. Aiden needed a safe place to stay.

Hope's offer came to mind. Maybe he did have other options. Aiden had really connected with the quiet woman who knew exactly what to say to comfort him last night. What wasn't to like about Hope? She was warm, friendly, and beautiful. But surely he couldn't ask a stranger to watch his nephew? Could he? No, Hope had a job, too. Just like he did. And the boy's grandmother was willing to watch him. What harm would it do?

His sister in her drugged-out state flashed in his mind. If Ginny held a grudge, that was on her. She had made some horrible choices. Now these were the consequences she was going to have to live with. Heck, she was blessed to still be on this side of the dirt. If Travis hadn't administered Narcan when he did, she might have died right in front of Aiden.

Dismissing the thoughts that were twisting his gut, Travis pulled out of the parking space. The kid didn't have a choice.

"Grandma has a phone in the kitchen that I can use?" Aiden asked, apparently seeking confirmation.

"Yep, I'll show you it when we get there." Travis looked in the rearview mirror. Aiden rested his chin on his new Lego set. His brown eyes radiated his apprehension. He had probably been lied to so many times that he didn't know who to trust. It broke Travis's heart, but he could relate to the child in a way most couldn't.

Travis had been that little boy. His father was mean.

Meaner when he was drunk or high. His mother wasn't any help because she was also afraid of his wrath and fell into a spiral of drug use, too. His mother was an embarrassment when she came into school with stale-smelling clothes and glassy eyes. It wasn't until Travis met the school resource officer that he found a mentor and a path to the future. His father was enraged when he learned about that development. How could his only son look up to a man who had arrested his father on various occasions for a multitude of offenses: drunk and disorderly, disturbing the peace, driving under the influence?

When his father announced that he was disowning his son, Travis had bit back the laughter that was echoing in his head. Disowning him? *Ha.* The dump of a house was the only thing his father owned and he hadn't even worked for it. He had inherited it from his parents.

Travis disliked the person he was around his family. After he graduated from high school, his parents divorced. His mother had found sobriety and Jesus, not necessarily in that order. So, when his dad left this world after a night of heavy drinking and drugging, Ginny inherited the house and his father's propensity for addiction. Yet Travis had not gotten away entirely. His sense of obligation had him coming back. To help Ginny. And now her son.

"What if she doesn't let me use the phone?" Aiden asked, his voice quivering. Travis imagined he was sitting there, conjuring all the what ifs. He was a smart, thoughtful little boy.

"You can use the phone. I promise. Grandma is very old-school. She still has a landline. Right there on the wall."

"Landline?" He scrunched up his little face, clearly confused.

"Yes, anyone in the house can use them. Just pick it up and call me. Anytime."

"Okay," he whispered, seemingly not convinced. "Maybe you should get me a cell phone." There was a hopeful note to his tone. Apparently, this had not been the first time this child asked for a cell phone. "I could keep it in my pocket. For emergencies."

Normally, Travis would be opposed to a child having a cell phone, but in Aiden's case it wasn't a bad idea. "We'll see. But for now, there's a phone in the kitchen."

When they got to his mother's senior apartment complex, Travis's doubts began to grow. Maybe this wasn't a good idea. His mother had a sharp tongue, and Aiden didn't need to hear any of her snide comments about his mother.

The last time they had been here was Easter. By all accounts, six months ago Ginny had been doing well. Everyone thought she had been on the wagon for the past two years. At the time, she had left Kerry home—that should have been the first clue that he was spiraling. When their mother started in on her daughter's husband and how he was worthless, just like Ginny's dad, his sister had packed up and left, forcing Aiden to miss the community Easter egg hunt. It gutted Travis that most of their family gatherings had some element of drama in them. Couldn't a kid just be a kid?

Travis climbed out of the truck and opened the back door. "Ready, buddy?"

The little boy's chest heaved up and down, as if he had to take a large breath to get up the nerve. Inwardly Travis shook his head. Kids his age shouldn't be dealing with this kind of stress. Travis grabbed Cujo's leash and they headed toward his mother's.

"Hello there!" His mother stood in the doorway of the shared hallway with her hands clutched to her chest. "Look how big you're getting, Aiden." Her smile slid from her face. "Oh, you're outgrowing your clothes." She met Travis's gaze.

66

"Your sister has him in floods. Goodness." They were hardly floods, but rather joggers that had slid up his calf.

Unfazed by his mother's critical comments, Cujo jumped up, planting his paws on her wool pants. She held up her hands in horror and backed away. The dog came right back at her, thinking she was playing a game.

"Off!" Travis said, grabbing the dog's collar. "Good boy."

His mother pursed her lips, but she didn't say anything, probably because she had already agreed to the dog and she didn't like to be proven wrong.

Travis had hoped he'd make it through the front door before his blood pressure skyrocketed. Oh man, this was not a good idea. He was stuck between the proverbial rock and a hard place, and unfortunately, Aiden was about to get smooshed.

"How are you, Mother?" Travis gave her a perfunctory kiss on the cheek, still holding the dog back. She smelled of cigarette smoke and coffee.

"I'm fine," his mother said, sounding exhausted and like she was about to get into all the reasons she wasn't fine, including the dog jumping around her feet. She held out her hand and Aiden dipped his head and wandered over to her. She pushed a lock of her grandson's hair out of his face, judgment etched in her twisted features.

Travis needed to get his nephew settled, but he feared the longer he stayed, the more likely he'd have a confrontation with his mother. That wouldn't benefit anyone. "Aiden," he said, cheerily, "let's get your things. Can you watch Cujo?" He handed off the leash to his mother.

"What a silly name," she muttered before talking baby talk to the dog while leading him inside.

His nephew's face brightened a fraction, perhaps remembering his new toys. As they stood by the open trunk, with his mother out of earshot, Travis whispered, "Grandma Hart loves you. She really does." He believed that in his heart, even though she had a rough way of showing it.

"What are floods?" Aiden asked. The innocence and sincerity in his eyes crushed Travis's heart.

He decided to be direct. "Pants that are too short." He crouched down to get on eye level with his nephew. "Grandma isn't up on the current fashion. You are not wearing floods."

Aiden bent over and tugged the cuffs on his pants down over his white socks. Then he straightened and took one of the bags from Travis. Together they climbed the stairs to the second-story apartment.

Upon seeing the shopping bags, his mother said, "You're going to spoil that child."

Anger pulsed in Travis's chest. Why did his mother have to make a comment about everything? If his mother understood the full context of what had happened—what Aiden had witnessed—she'd never accuse this child of being spoiled. But if Travis told her how his sister had been living, his mother would use that against her daughter in a nonproductive way. Interacting with his mother was like balancing on a tightrope. He had to determine what to share, or not share, never knowing if he was going to make it to the other side without plunging to his death because of a misstep.

"Why don't we put your things in the guest bedroom," he said to Aiden, then looked over at his mother. "Is that okay?"

His mother hitched a shoulder, as if to say, *Whatever*. Travis sensed her growing agitation. Perhaps she resented Travis taking charge. But he had to get the child settled before he left for work so he led him to the bedroom.

Travis sat down on the edge of the bed and patted it. His nephew joined him, his little sneakers sticking straight out in front of him. "Can you think of anything else you need?"

His nephew looked around, taking in the bland white walls and the floral bedspread. It wasn't exactly a boy's bedroom, but it was clean and that was the main thing. Travis unzipped the duffel bag and pulled out a stuffed bear. He held it out. "I got your stuffy."

Aiden's eyes widened. He grabbed the bear and tucked it under his chin. "Dad says I'm not a baby anymore."

"Of course you're not. But everyone needs a stuffy after a tough day." Travis smiled. "Right?"

Aiden nodded and stroked the bear's back. Meanwhile Cujo wandered into the room and made it his business to smell each and every square inch of the place.

"I have muffins." The singsong quality of his mother's voice annoyed Travis. Probably because he'd spent his childhood assessing her moods. Was she happy? How long would it last? If not, would he be the subject of her anger?

Travis patted his nephew's little knee. "Ready, buddy?" He held out his hand and Aiden took it.

When they got to the kitchen, his mother was taking muffins from a brown bag and setting them out on a plate. "I hope you like blueberry muffins."

Aiden nodded enthusiastically. "I do."

Travis's mother placed a muffin on a paper plate and smiled broadly. She winked at Travis as if to say, *See, everything will be completely fine.*

Maybe Travis was being too critical. Maybe his mother deserved another shot.

People change, right?

CHAPTER 9

*L*ater that afternoon, Hope took her burner phone and walked around to the back toward the barn on the B&B property. The barn was updated and in good condition. According to Mary, animals hadn't seen the inside of the structure in a long time. They used it more as a showpiece for the guests. To add an Amish flavor, she claimed. As if the Amish women working at the B&B weren't enough. Sometimes they even set up a table and chairs for a romantic dinner for couples. Hope couldn't help but wonder what kind of success Mary, who was very entrepreneurial, would have if she didn't have the constraints of being an Amish woman.

Shaking away her meandering thoughts, Hope sat down on a hay bale with her eye to the door so as not to be overheard. She dialed a friend from home whose number she had committed to memory.

"Hello?" Skylar answered, her voice hesitant, as if she was bracing herself for a pitch for an extended car warranty for a car she didn't own. Hope figured she deserved that since her number was probably coming up as unknown. She was simply grateful that the woman answered.

"Skylar, it's me." A rush of goose bumps washed over Hope, as if she had broken a pact with herself. When she left Buffalo, she had vowed to cut off all ties to stay safe. But after last night, after being reminded firsthand how a life can be forever changed in an instant, she needed to reach out to her past. Check on the one living person who meant the world to her.

"Harper?" the young woman said, an air of disbelief in her tone. "Is it really you? OMG, you really did it."

"I did." Hope's heart thundered in her ears. Skylar had been the one person she told that if she disappeared, she didn't want to be found. That she had to escape Derek. Heart beating wildly, Hope feared she wouldn't be able to hear her friend over the line. "Don't say my name out loud." Was she being overly paranoid? No, after her experiences, she could never be too careful. "Are you by yourself?" She didn't want to put Skylar in jeopardy if Derek thought the nursing student could track down his ex.

"Yes, I'm home alone. I'm studying. Where *are* you? I was so worried."

"I'm fine. I'd rather not say where I am."

"Right," Skylar said. "This way that jerk can't ask me." Skylar worked as an aide at the nursing home where Miss June lived. That would be a likely connection that Derek would pursue.

"Exactly." Hope crossed an arm over her middle and smiled, imagining the young woman finally taking the classes she needed for a nursing degree. Hope would have loved a redo when it came to college. "What class did you sign up for?"

"Anatomy. It's one of the pre-reqs to get into the nursing program."

"That's awesome, Sky."

"Okay, okay, enough about me. Tell me about you?"

"Not much to say. I'm safe." The sound of a truck barreling down the country road rumbled in the distance. "I'm weighing my options."

Skylar lowered her voice. "Derek tracked me down at the college bookstore. He wanted to know where you were."

He was stalking Hope's friend. Just as she had feared. Her stomach twisted. "I'm so sorry you had to get involved with this." She bit her lower lip. "Maybe I shouldn't have called."

"No worries." Hope could imagine her young friend waving her hand with her black-painted nails. "I told him I had no idea what was going on. Good idea that you didn't tell me your plan."

"Plan?" Hope laughed. "I didn't have much of one."

"You're really okay?" Skylar asked.

"I'm hanging in there." She hated that she couldn't share the details of her life with someone from her past.

"Will you ever come home?"

Hope stood and brushed the bits of hay from her jeans. Through the open barn door she could see the large windows on the back of the B&B. "I've been living day to day." She couldn't go back if Derek was looking for her. Would he ever stop? He was a spiteful man.

"Um, I hate to tell you this, but Miss June had a stroke."

"Oh, no. How is she?" A knot twisted in her gut. Miss June was the closest thing she had to a mother after her own died.

"Miss June's in the rehab unit, but her daughter thinks they're going to have to move her to the memory care side of the nursing home." Skylar's voice got quiet. "I'm sorry. But don't worry, I'll check on her. You can call me anytime for updates."

Calling for updates and seeing Miss June in person were two far different things.

The sun slicing through the wood slats of the barn made Hope feel dizzy. She plowed her hand through her hair. Tears burned the back of Hope's eyes but her cheeks remained dry. She had already expended all her tears. She bit her lower lip.

The sudden loss of her mom had been awful, but it was made worse because Hope hadn't realized she was dying. She never got to say goodbye. She never got to say all the things she should have told her mom. Instead, she had been a typical prickly pre-teen, causing her mom grief, only to find her only family dead in her bed one morning. The guilt haunted her, even now.

Hope had replayed events of her mother's last year of life. Her mother's mood seemed to darken after their trip to Hunters Ridge. It wasn't until Hope stumbled upon the photograph of Hope, Mary and her mother in an old book of her mother's about a year ago that she started planning a trip. Had Hope known back then that the trip to Hunters Ridge was going to be her escape from her ex? Or just a way to revisit a past that included her mom?

She couldn't be sure. But here she was.

"Are you going to come see her?" Skylar asked expectantly. "You can stay at my apartment. I'd love for you to see it." Her friend's speech sped up when she got excited. "No one has to know you're here."

Hope frowned. "As much as I want to, it's not safe." She had to force the words through the emotion in her throat. "Please let Miss June know I love her."

"Okay..." The disappointment in Skylar's tone was palpable. "Will you call me again?"

"Yes." She'd try. "It might be from a different number because I have one of those disposable phones."

Skylar sighed heavily. "This is some messed up stuff."

"It is." The walls of the barn suddenly felt close; the earthy smells cloying in her nose. Hope strolled outside and tipped her face up to the sun. The breeze felt heavenly on her arms. "Good luck in school." She lowered her head and tented her hand over her eyes. The country was blissful. "I'm really proud of you."

"I'm proud of *you*," her friend said. Hope could hear a smile in Skylar's voice.

"Maybe someday we can celebrate us."

"I'd really like that," Skylar said.

"Me, too." A knot of indecision tightened in Hope's chest. She had made tremendous strides to get herself out of a horrible situation. And she had been successful. But her current situation left her in a sort of limbo.

Could she let go completely of her past to bravely move into the future? To really live her life? Or would she forever be hiding in the shadows for fear her past would reach out and snatch her back?

CHAPTER 10

*L*ater that afternoon, Travis went to visit his sister in the hospital. Since it was Sunday, the halls were a little quieter than usual. He supposed that wasn't a bad thing for a hospital.

He punched the blue square with a wheelchair on it and the door to his sister's wing flung open. He was generally a confident guy but dealing with his family took him back in time. He thought he had escaped the drama of his childhood.

Darn, his nerves were humming.

"Good afternoon." He nodded at the nurse sitting behind a desk and she returned his greeting with a smile.

He had no idea which Ginny he'd see. The remorseful one who'd be crying and pleading how she had messed up and was so sorry. Or perhaps the "woe is me Ginny" complaining how life beat her down to the point she had no choice but to numb herself. Then there was the angry version of his big sister. The one who'd be pissed at the world—or him specifically—for saving her and landing her in the hospital because she'd rather be dead.

Travis hated that it was only a sense of obligation that

propelled him forward. It was strange that his sister ignited the same fight-or-flight response as a dangerous middle-of-the-night response to a call. He'd had hundreds of them as a sheriff's deputy. But family was different. His family, at least. He couldn't objectively write up an incident report and walk away. Or he could, but then Aiden would be the one to lose the most. So, in the end, he was doing all this for Aiden. The kid needed family. And if Ginny wasn't up for it, then he would step up.

Travis slowed outside Ginny's door to make sure she was alone. He didn't want a confrontation with his sister in front of witnesses. He could hear her talking. She sounded agitated. He peered into the room and found her sitting up, waving her hand attached to an IV, and yelling into the phone.

"No, that's not going to happen." A vein was bulging under the papery-thin flesh on her forehead. "No way."

Travis glanced toward the nurses' station, and the nurse he had greeted was looking in his direction with a scowl on her face. Ginny was going to have to tone it down. Travis slipped into the room and put his index finger to his lips and gestured toward the door with his head. Ginny rolled her eyes and her lips twitched. Her face flushed, probably a combination of embarrassment and anger.

Ginny ended the call and tossed the phone onto her bed. It landed on her thighs then slid down.

"You okay?" Travis asked.

Ginny hiked a shoulder.

"Who was that?" he asked.

Just as expected, the nurse appeared in the doorway. "Everything okay in here?"

"Everything's fine." Travis waved at her and the nurse gave him a smile and an eyebrow raise and left.

"They're so uptight in here." Ginny laid back and dragged

her hand through her hair. Her coloring was still off and her arms were thinner than he remembered.

Travis shrugged. What did she expect in a hospital? But bringing it up wouldn't help his cause. "Who was on the phone?"

"That's what you're going to ask me? Who was that?" She attempted to mimic him in a high, nasally voice that did nothing other than to make her look silly.

Travis let out a long, frustrated breath. He and his sister had always had a strained relationship. She was three years older, and in kid years that was a lifetime. She'd gone from being a nagging mom with the absence of their own, straight to the irresponsible sister who'd discovered that misbehaving was one sure way to get their parents' attention.

He planted a kiss on her forehead and started over. "How are you feeling?"

"Like I got hit by a Mack truck." She rubbed the heel of her hand to her chest. "My stupid neighbor called complaining about the stuff piled on the front porch. As if I don't have bigger problems."

"She's probably not aware you're in the hospital."

"Oh, she is. She asked if she could clean up the yard while I was here." The deep lines around Ginny's pursed lips made her appear older than she was. Smoking did that to a person.

Travis pulled up a chair and sat down.

Before he had a chance to say anything, Ginny held up her hand and closed her eyes. "Stop, little brother. I don't want to hear it. I don't want to be yelled at by anyone else."

Anger churned in his gut. "Okay, if you're so smart, tell me what I was going to say."

"You're going to say 'back off the drugs' and I already know that. Let it rest already. I'm trying. It's hard. You wouldn't understand."

Travis tilted his head. "If you don't want to make any changes for you, then make them for Aiden."

She crossed her arms over her frail body and sighed. Her lower lip began to quiver. "I said I was trying."

"Ginny, I'm here to help," Travis said. "Don't shut me out."

"I don't need your help. I never have." Her words came out clipped, defiant, lacking in self-awareness. "Kerry and I are Aiden's parents. We'll manage just fine."

"You'll manage just fine? Is that what you're doing here?"

"I messed up. It won't happen again," Ginny said, as if she was talking about adding bleach to a load of darks. Yeah, a mistake, but nothing lost other than ruined clothes. Now her drug addiction was a high-stakes risk. She waved her fingers at him. "Kerry will take care of him until I get out of here. So yeah, we've got this covered."

Travis's pulse whooshed in his head. "Have you talked to Kerry?" He hated to use this as a gotcha moment, but his sister was a drug addict. And in her current state of denial, she had grown smug. He needed to put an end to it.

"It's not like I've been up to making calls."

"That's a no?" Travis asked, pushing to his feet.

"No, I haven't," she said forcefully. "I'm sure he'll be stopping by soon."

"Kerry will not be stopping by soon. Kerry will not be caring for Aiden."

His sister's face scrunched up, then slowly her jaw grew slack. "What in the world are you talking about?" Concern flashed in her eyes. The delicate skin under them was a blueish black. His sister needed a good detox program, a healthy diet, and a solid night of sleep. And unless she changed her attitude, she'd be getting none of those things.

"Kerry's in lockup."

"Lockup?" Ginny sat upright, her eyes wide. "Why? He had nothing to do with me ending up here. That's all on me.

Come on." Her tone had shifted from angry denial to panicked pleading.

"He was driving under the influence."

Ginny studied him a moment, then her eyes narrowed. "I don't believe you." Her tone grew accusatory. "You're punishing him. You're like Mom. You don't like him, so you had him pulled over." Ginny's eyes grew dark with an undercurrent of hatred.

His heart broke for her, but she needed the unvarnished truth. "Kerry plowed into the Wash & Go." He understood why his mother didn't care for Kerry. His negative influence had kept his sister in a loop of drug use, recovery, drug use. Lather, rinse, repeat.

"Where's Aiden?" Ginny asked, struggling to straighten her back. She looked petite in the hospital bed. "Where. Is. My. Son?"

Travis placed his hand on her leg. "Aiden is safe. He's with Mother."

Ginny's face crumbled and she folded in half and sobbed.

"This has to be the wake-up call, Ginny. Get well for Aiden."

His sister lifted her tear-stained face. "Please, can you take him in? Just until I kick this."

"I love Aiden, but I have to work. Someone must be with him. I'll go visit as much as I can."

"Mother will turn him against me. *Please.*" Her heartbreaking pleas got under his skin. "You have to."

"I'll support you in whatever way I can. Aiden is safe. And you need to go to rehab."

Ginny's lower lip quivered. She leaned back and closed her eyes. He had never seen his sister so defeated. After a heartbeat, she said, "When will Kerry get out?"

"I don't know." And he really didn't care.

Ginny's chest deflated.

"Even if he came home tonight, Aiden wouldn't be allowed to live in that house. It's uninhabitable," Travis said, inexplicably finding himself reasoning with her.

His proud big sister averted her gaze. "I've made a huge mess of things, haven't I?"

Travis took her hand. "I'll help you, but you have to want to help yourself, too."

"I do. I do," she added a second time for emphasis.

Travis smiled tightly. "Rest. I'll make a few phone calls to find a spot for you in rehab."

Ginny flopped back against the pillow, looking like she wanted to protest, but in that moment she had enough sense to remain quiet.

Travis squeezed her hand. "I'll talk to you later, okay? Rest."

She nodded. A single tear tracked down her cheek. Maybe, just maybe, she'd do the work she needed to do.

For Aiden.

CHAPTER 11

*T*ravis watched Hope pick a piece of bacon out of her club sandwich and popped it into her mouth. "Thanks for picking me up. I had to get out. Mary was having a few of her friends over and I didn't want to be the odd man out."

"I'm glad you called," Travis said, stirring the sugar in his coffee. The diner had some of the best coffee.

She scrunched up her pretty face. "Won't that keep you awake tonight?"

Travis set the spoon on the napkin. "Caffeine is not the thing that keeps me awake." Between his sister, nephew and job, he had trouble shutting off his brain.

"Perhaps I should have some coffee." She laughed, then dipped her head, letting her silky hair fall in a curtain down the side of her face.

Man, he was glad she had called him tonight. It had been completely unexpected. And fortunately for him, the sheriff had overscheduled the second shift so he'd volunteered to go home, only to get a last-minute phone call from the newest resident of Hunters Ridge. He considered it a lucky turn of events after all the bad news of late. "Want some? They make a great cup here."

"Oh, no. I was kidding. I'll take a rain check, though."

"Deal." He smiled and her cheeks grew pink.

She took a bite of her sandwich, then swiped a smudge of mayo from the corner of her mouth with her pinky. "Any updates on your sister?"

"She's agreed to go to rehab."

"That's good, right?" He wished he had the kind of hope that was reflected in her eyes.

"We've been here before. I pray Aiden is enough reason for her to get clean."

Hope tucked a strand of hair behind her ear. "He's a good kid. He really is."

"You were great with him." He dipped his spoon into his chicken noodle soup, blew on it a bit before putting it in his mouth. "I appreciate it."

"He's been through a lot." Her tone suggested she understood what he was going through.

There was so much he didn't know about her. Heck, he hardly knew anything about her save for her position at the B&B. "Can I ask you something?"

"I can't promise I'll answer," she said, setting the sandwich down on the plate and giving him a shy smile.

He held up his hand. "I don't mean to pry. I'd like to get to know you better, though."

She smiled tightly and he wished he knew what was going on in her pretty head.

"What brought you to Hunters Ridge?" Something flashed in the depths of her eyes.

"I needed a fresh start." She picked up her napkin and wiped her fingers. He waited her out. "I had a bad breakup."

"I'm sorry to hear that. Are you okay?"

She frowned and her lower lip began to quiver.

"What is it?"

"A woman who raised me after my mother died had a stroke. I'm worried I won't get to see her again." She swiped at a tear trailing down her cheek. "I'm sorry. I didn't mean to unload on you. You have enough going on."

He reached across the table and stopped short of taking her hand. He didn't want to scare her away right when she was starting to open up to him. "Don't feel that way. Do you have plans to go visit her?"

"I'd like to, but I don't have transportation."

"To Buffalo? I don't have to work until three tomorrow. I can take you."

Hope looked like she was about to refuse, but instead she said, "I'd like that."

"Okay, let me know what time to pick you up and I'll be there."

The next day, Hope buckled her seat belt and immediately doubted her decision. She was taking a huge chance going home to visit Miss June, but she hadn't been able to sleep most of the night thinking about her. She had to see the sweet woman.

"It's a beautiful fall day for a ride," Travis said. He had picked her up in his civilian vehicle and she was glad for that. She didn't need anything connecting her to Hunters Ridge—that is, if someone was paying attention.

Hope felt a smile tugging on her lips. "Ah, you're too kind. I totally realize it's a huge inconvenience." She was grateful for his generosity in offering her a ride, yet she hadn't been fully honest with him. She had neglected to tell him that her ex was a stalker. She wasn't ready to share everything, especially her biggest failure.

Hope always felt like she was responsible for the mess she was in. Like, what kind of idiot falls for a psychopath? Shouldn't she have seen the signs earlier? Intellectually, she knew these kinds of men were great at hiding who they were until it was too late. But emotionally, she flogged herself for not being more careful. *Stupid, stupid, stupid.* She should have never gotten herself into this situation.

"I'll make this a quick visit. In and out. I promise," she said, her nerves growing tauter as the mile markers ticked by.

"It's fine. We can grab some lunch, if you'd like. I don't have to work until three p.m., and my mother said she and Aiden were going to walk to the park with Cujo."

Alarm shot through her. She couldn't spend a minute longer in Buffalo than was necessary. "I couldn't possibly take up your whole day." She tried to sound breezy, as if her very life didn't depend on getting in and out without being seen.

"We can play it by ear."

"Um, sure." She hated to sound ungrateful.

As they got closer to the rehab center, Hope had to breathe in and out slowly in a futile effort to remain calm. It was tough to pretend she wasn't having a panic attack when every inch of her skin was crawling with nerves.

Maybe I shouldn't have come.

Stupid. Stupid. Stupid.

When they pulled into the lot, she was wound so tight she wanted to spring out of the car. She felt trapped. Confined. Anxious. She swallowed down her emotions and forced a cheery demeanor. "Do you mind waiting here? I'll be right back."

"No problem. I'll be here. Take your time."

"Thank you."

Hope walked through the main door and the hairs on the

back of her neck prickled to life. She glanced over her shoulder. Travis was distracted by his phone. Nothing seemed off, at least by first glance. Yet she strode into the lobby on high alert.

She scanned the faces of elderly folks in wheelchairs, their family or attendants, and a few staff members with ID lanyards draped around their necks. Tears burned at the back of her throat at the thought of sweet Miss June not being able to live out her days in her cozy home filled with photographs of the smiling faces of all the foster kids she had taken in over the years. Before Hope's mom died, she had visited her neighbor's home, and as an only child she was jealous that the woman had such a large family. Little did Hope know, until her own mother died and her (not so smiling) face got a place on the mantel, that Miss June had been a well-loved foster mom, and all those kids had been part of the foster system. Hope would have rather had her mom, but she was always grateful Miss June had stepped into her life. Until recently, Hope had been good about staying in touch, just like most of the other kids.

Oh, how she had wanted to be another of the kindly woman's success stories. Instead, she had been another stupid statistic.

"May I help you?" Hope snapped out of her spiraling thoughts to find a woman behind a desk stationed near a set of elevators staring at her.

"Yes, I'm here to see June Baranski." Hope's voice broke and the attendant glanced up at her briefly before returning her attention to her screen.

She reached up and patted a sheet on the desk. "Sign in here. She's only allowed one guest at a time."

"I came alone."

The woman nodded. "If someone is in with her, please wait until they leave." She peeled a purple visitor sticker from the roll and handed it to Hope. "Baranski is on the second floor."

The woman smiled tightly and Hope signed the register with her fake name in handwriting that would make a doctor proud, then turned toward the elevators, feeling a niggle of guilt for being deceitful.

The entire time Hope was waiting for the elevator, she couldn't shake a horrible sensation that someone was watching her.

You're fine. You're fine.

Hope fought her unease—*it's just because you're back in Buffalo*. It was a risk, but a necessary one. She'd never forgive herself if the woman died and Hope never got to say her goodbyes. She was still living with the regret of not understanding the gravity of her mother's illness. And never getting to say goodbye to her.

The doors pinged open on the second floor. Hope followed the signs to Miss June's room. She felt a little silly glancing over her shoulder and around each corner. The only person she encountered, besides elderly patients in wheelchairs, was a young nurse dressed in blue scrubs sorting through various meds.

When Hope reached the room, she froze in the doorway at the sight of the woman who had been the closest thing she'd had to a grandmother. Under her colorful bedspread— presumably brought from home—her frame looked frail. Hope had to swallow her emotions, afraid if she started to cry she'd never stop.

She stood by Miss June's bed for a long time, watching the woman's chest rise and fall. Her long white hair that was usually braided and looped over the crown of her head was loose and looked like it needed a good wash. A coarse gray hair grew unchecked from her chin. Miss June had always taken great pride in her appearance.

"Miss June," Hope whispered, eager to see the woman's beautiful blue eyes, but also not wanting to disturb her rest. "Miss June, it's me"—her voice squeaked—"Harper."

"She sleeps most of the time."

Hope's heart jolted out of her chest at the approach of a young woman in blue scrubs. The one she had passed who had been sorting medicine earlier. How long had she been standing there? Hope had to blink a few times to gather her thoughts. "Is she…okay?" It seemed like a silly question.

"She's comfortable. Physical rehab seems to take it out of her, though." The young woman, who was probably about her age, give or take, pressed her lips together and gave her a sympathetic smile. "Due to privacy laws, I can't say much more…" The woman's voice trailed off and Hope felt her face heating. "Are you family?"

"She was my foster mom."

The woman reached into the large pockets on the front of her scrubs and snagged a cell phone. Before Hope had a chance to protest, the woman had taken a photo of her. Her throat went dry. The woman smiled. "Mrs. Baranski is having trouble with her memory. I'll show her your photo when she wakes up." She glanced at the screen, then slipped the phone back into her pocket. "Your name is Harper?"

"Um…" Hope's breath grew ragged.

"I heard you talking to her," the nurse said, by way of explanation.

I shouldn't have come. It's a mistake. Then a more rational voice: *Would Derek track me down through my former foster mom?* Despite the absurdity of it, she had her concerns. She wouldn't put anything past that jerk. But she also wanted to bring Miss June some comfort. Maybe a harmless photo would help.

"She goes by Miss June," Hope said, doing her best to keep her voice calm, like fighting a swarm of anxious bees buzzing over every inch of her body. "She never married and always corrected people when they called her Mrs. She was funny like that. I mean, she had a great sense of humor. She took in a ton of foster kids."

The woman's gaze narrowed with curiosity. "She talks a lot about her kids. She's had a wonderful life."

A squirrely feeling made Hope want to flee. *You're being paranoid.* She cleared her throat. "Yes, she has. She's a wonderful person."

"I wish she was awake. It would do her wonders to see you," the staff member said. "I'll be sure to make a note that she prefers to be called Miss June." She giggled. "We've probably been stressing her out without realizing it. Miss June, it is." The woman raised her eyebrows expectantly. "Harper, what's your last name?"

"She'll know who Harper is."

"Of course," the woman said and stared at her. She apparently had no intention of leaving. If Hope had wanted to bare her soul to Miss June while she lay sleeping, the moment had passed.

"It was nice to meet you," Hope said.

"Will you be back? I'm sure Miss June would love to see you when she's not so tired."

Hope let her eyes land on Miss June's face and she had a sudden urge to sob. "I'll be back. Please let her know I was here."

"Leave your cell phone number." The cheap drawer on the rollaway food tray had to be jigged open. The woman grabbed a piece of paper and pen. "I'm sure she'd love to talk to you, although, she has trouble hearing sometimes."

"Oh, I don't…" For some reason, Hope neglected to tell her that she already had a friend who worked here. However, she didn't want anyone to be able to make any other connections to her. It was safer that way. For everyone.

The woman handed her the paper. "Write it down. What can it hurt? Once her brain has time to heal, it's important that she stay engaged."

"True." Hope jotted down her number and set it on Miss June's food tray that sat unused off to the side. "For when she wakes up."

The woman smiled. "Now that's the spirit."

Hope felt like she had somehow let that interaction get out of control. Perhaps she was being paranoid. Perhaps she had a right to be concerned. "I better get going," she said. "Have a nice afternoon."

"You, too," the young woman called out after her.

Hope still couldn't shake her unease. She took the stairs instead of the elevator and breathed a sigh of relief when she stepped out into the fall afternoon. The refreshing breeze set her back into the moment.

Her eyes scanned the parking lot for Travis's truck, but she didn't have to wait long. He zipped up to the curb and leaned over and pushed open her door a fraction.

"How'd it go?" Immediately, his strong presence and the hint of his aftershave already made her feel better. Secure.

"Miss June sleeps a lot. Staff could only tell me that the stroke has likely affected both her physical health and her memory. They won't know how much about the latter until the brain heals. It takes time." Hope stared out the passenger window at the entrance of the rehabilitation center, fearing she'd never get to see Miss June alive and well again. Or maybe she would. Maybe she'd find Hope's phone number and call.

Leaving her number had been a good idea, right? It was a burner phone. It couldn't be tracked. Could it? Had Hope allowed her emotions to preempt her common sense? She didn't want to have to run again.

Stupid. Stupid. Stupid.

The glass front doors slid open and the staff member who had been in Miss June's room came out pushing a patient, perhaps taking advantage of the warm afternoon. Hope lifted a hand and waved. The woman stared right through her. *Didn't she see me?*

Hope shifted in her seat to face Travis, uneasiness creeping up and heating her cheeks. "Let's go."

CHAPTER 12

*T*ravis couldn't help but notice that Hope seemed excessively fidgety in the passenger seat on the drive back to Hunters Ridge from Buffalo. They had made pleasant small talk here and there about sights on the side of the road, the B&B where she worked, and her friend Miss June. But it had all been superficial, touching on subjects any two strangers could discuss, which they technically were. His intuition told him she was hiding something, but he feared if he pressed, she'd shut down. He decided to go at it indirectly.

"Don't you have any family or friends who could check on Miss June for you?" Travis asked, cutting her a sideways glance before turning his attention back to the road.

"Well, one of the aides called me to tell me about her stroke. But Miss June may have to move to a memory care facility, and I don't know anyone there." She crossed her arms over her thin frame. "I won't have any way of checking on her."

"I can bring you back whenever you want," Travis offered.

"I can't keep imposing," she said, her tentative tone

suggesting that wasn't the primary reason she was staying away.

What is she hiding?

"You grew up in Buffalo?" Meaning, she had to have friends, if not family there to help her out. He wasn't usually nosy, but she made him curious. He wanted to know everything about her, even as he sensed she had a protective wall around her heart.

He could relate.

"I did," Hope said quietly. "My mother died when I was twelve." She picked at something invisible on her jeans. "That's when I went to live with Miss June. She's a foster parent."

"You spent your teen years in the foster system."

"Yeah." She let out a long sigh. "It wasn't awful. Miss June was my neighbor. I knew her for years before my mom died. Thankfully, I stayed with Miss June until I aged out." She cleared her throat. "Even after that, I visited her. She had moved to a senior apartment." There was a wistful quality to her voice. "I miss her."

"What brought you to Hunters Ridge?" The question seemed like an obvious segue, but out of the corner of his eye he saw her flinch.

"The job."

"At the B&B?" he pressed.

Hope shifted in her seat and bent her head slightly and scratched the small space between her eyebrows. "I appreciate the ride, I really do, but what's with the third degree?" She had answered a few questions last night over dinner, but he had hoped she'd answer more today. Maybe that had been wishful thinking.

Travis kept his gaze on the thruway ahead of them. He tapped on the steering wheel with his thumb. "Sorry. I guess I'm curious by nature. Didn't mean to pry." Trying to learn more about this mysterious, beautiful woman had become a challenge, but he also wanted to respect her privacy.

A worry had been nagging at him, but he didn't want to push her. She seemed skittish and she obviously was afraid of something or someone, unless he was misreading her aloofness as something sinister. It wasn't any of his business, anyway.

The phone rang and he answered it on speaker.

"Uncle Travis." Aiden's shaky voice floated into the cabin of his truck. "Can you come get me?" There was a shuffling sound coming over the phone that suggested he was trying to keep the phone call a secret.

"What's up, bud?" Travis glanced over at his passenger and shrugged.

"I don't like it here." Each word was enunciated around a shuddering sob.

"Are you hurt?" Travis asked, alarm heating his skin.

"No..."

"Then what's wrong, buddy? Where's Grandma?"

"She threw out my Legos."

Unreasonable anger heated Travis's cheeks. "What happened?"

"I was playing with them on the carpet and she stepped on one. She said lots of bad words."

"Boy, that must have hurt," Travis tried to rationalize. But how could his mother throw out a kid's toy, especially after everything Aiden had been through? "Maybe she put them away until later. Are you sure she threw them out?"

Aiden sniffed over the line and Travis could imagine him shrugging like he always did. "She told me I was an idiot. Like my dad."

Travis plowed a hand through his hair. "Listen buddy, Grandma sometimes says stuff she doesn't mean when she's angry." It was no excuse, but what else could he say?

Ginny. He had promised his sister he'd look out for her son. Just because he had a roof over his head didn't mean he was safe.

"I don't like it here. Can you come and get me?"

Travis ran a hand over his scratchy jaw.

"I can watch myself. Please. Come get me. I'm a big boy. Mommy says so."

"I have to work tonight." Travis could only imagine how often this child had been left to his own devices. Maybe he could put in for vacation days, but it didn't solve the issue of his shift that started in a few hours. "I'll see about getting some time off work. Do you think you can manage one more night?"

"She locks Cujo in the closet."

So much for taking him for walks in the park. Travis's growing anger pulsed in his head. *Is Mom lying to me again? Just like she did to her two school-aged kids because she was too drugged up to know or care about the truth.*

"Your grandmother locks your puppy in the closet?" A ticking started in his head, and he almost didn't feel Hope's hand on his arm.

"I can sit with your nephew while you work," she whispered, probably so Aiden wouldn't overhear.

That would be a perfect solution. "Hold on a second," he said to his nephew, then to Hope, "Are you sure? Don't you have to work at the B&B?"

"There aren't any guests scheduled until the weekend. Mary has me deep cleaning each room, one by one, but that can keep. I'm sure of it." Hope's mood seemed to brighten. Perhaps she was looking forward to a change of pace.

Thank you, he mouthed. Gosh, he could kiss her right now.

Hope was about to say something else when he held up his

finger in a hold-on-a-minute gesture. "Aiden..." He checked the time "...I'll be there in thirty minutes to pick you up. Don't say anything to your grandmother. I want it to be a surprise." His nephew had already been through enough without dealing with any blowback from his controlling grandmother.

Travis had never been able to stand up to her or his father when he was a kid. But he wasn't a kid anymore and he refused to let her plow over her only grandson.

Two hours later, Travis and Hope had his nephew set up on the couch with his favorite movie, and more importantly, Cujo at his side. The small black and white puppy had his snout pressed on the little guy's lap. Aiden's eyelids grew heavy. It was unlikely he'd make it through the movie.

Travis's mother had grumbled that *she* could take care of Aiden, but strangely enough she didn't put up much of an argument when Travis offered to take the child off her hands. Perhaps she only liked the idea of spending time with her only grandson. And there was no way in good conscience that Travis could leave Aiden and Cujo in an unhappy situation.

He and Hope were in the kitchen putting together a tray with cheese, fruit and crackers. Hope cut up the cheddar block.

Travis gently touched her hand, making her pause to look at him. "I can't thank you enough." Both of their gazes went to the back of the child's head as if simultaneously wondering how much he could overhear.

"My pleasure. I'm looking forward to curling up on the couch and relaxing." She smiled, a distant look in her eyes. "I haven't watched TV since I moved here."

"The Amish have always been my neighbors but I still find their way of life fascinating. It must be peaceful."

Hope shrugged. "It leaves a person alone with their thoughts, which isn't always a good thing." Her cheeks colored and she quickly added, "There, I think that's probably enough cheese."

Travis smiled. "About earlier…"

A thin line creased the center of her brow and he had to fight the urge to smooth it with the pad of his thumb. "Earlier?" Her pretty blue eyes darted around, as if she was trying to anticipate where the conversation was headed.

"Yeah, in the car. I didn't mean to ask so many questions about your past."

She lowered her gaze and picked up the knife and continued cutting slices of cheese. Aww, man, he had put his foot in it again.

"I shouldn't…" he added, suddenly at a loss for words. In his job he was used to peppering suspects and victims alike with questions until they were compelled to answer. Sometimes he forgot how to be subtle. And caring.

Then, apparently having sympathy for him, she set the knife down and turned to face him. "Your instincts are right, but I'm not ready to answer your questions." Shaking her head, she turned back to the task at hand. "I don't know who I can trust."

Her statement should have pained him, but it was fair. She didn't know much about him. They had only met a couple days ago, but it felt like longer. "When you're ready. I'm here," he said. "I hope someday you can trust me."

"I appreciate that," she said, sounding a bit too businesslike.

He had no interest in pressing her, so he grabbed his nephew's favorite water bottle and filled it up. "Looks like you and Aiden are in for a Harry Potter marathon," he said, more than a bit envious.

"Are you sure his mom would be okay with us watching this? Aren't some of the parts too scary for him?" Hope asked.

"Ha, the kid has experienced far scarier things in life. Harry is a great escape." A knot of emotion tightened in his gut. "His mom and I were obsessed with the books when we were kids. Ginny would absolutely be okay with this. Thank you for offering to help me out."

"You're welcome." She opened the fridge and placed the cheese on the shelf and muttered to no one in particular, "I could use an escape, too."

Questions collided on the tip of Travis's tongue, but he'd have to be patient. He'd have to wait until Hope was good and ready to tell him what had brought her to Hunters Ridge, or risk alienating her altogether.

CHAPTER 13

*H*ope and Aiden had gotten into a routine each afternoon after his uncle went to work. They decided it would be easier if Hope babysat Aiden at the B&B so that she could also complete her other responsibilities. Turned out the kid was a big helper. Until he pooped himself out.

Hope gently covered Aiden with a crocheted blanket. The little boy had fallen asleep almost as soon as he finished his dinner. He'd had a busy afternoon helping Hope and Ada sweep out the barn behind the B&B. This weekend the weather was supposed to be nice, and Mary planned to serve appetizers there for the two couples who had reservations.

Hope crouched down and petted Cujo's head. The dog followed Aiden around, as if he could sense the child needed him. "What a good boy," she cooed. "What a very good boy."

"Would you like me to take him out?"

Hope glanced over her shoulder to find Ada standing there. When Hope met her gaze, Ada rushed into the room with the dog's leash. Cujo got up and danced around the hem of her dress excitedly.

"That would be great. Are you sure you don't mind?" Hope asked as she did a quick tidy of the living room.

"Not at all." Ada tapped her hands together quietly, so as not to disturb Aiden. "Let's go, Cujo." She spun and the dog happily followed her. She stopped in the doorway and hooked on the leash.

Mary came up behind her daughter and smiled. "Make sure you pick up any poop on the lawn. I don't need guests giving me a one-star review on Yelp because they ruined their expensive shoes."

Hope laughed. "How do you know about Yelp?" It was an online review site.

Mary pushed a stray hair off her forehead and lifted her chin with a dramatic flair. "I may be Amish," she said in a haughty voice, "but I do not live under a rock."

Hope laughed and was about to ask Mary if she ever considered leaving the Amish to become an even more successful businesswoman, but she decided that was a far too personal question. Her relationship with Mary had been growing closer and she didn't want to risk offending her. "You have a wonderful business here."

"*Gott* has blessed me for sure." Mary seemed to be staring at Hope in a strange way, then shook her head dismissively and turned her gaze on Aiden with his cheek pressed against the thin gray fabric.

The couch was the only piece of upholstered furniture in the house. Ada had explained that some Amish districts didn't allow it at all. So many different rules—Hope wondered how they kept track.

"Nothing as precious as watching a child sleep," Mary said, a soft smile on her lips.

Hope followed the woman's gaze to Aiden. His long lashes swept his cheeks, and she felt her heart stir. It wasn't that she longed for children—not that she was against the idea either. She just hadn't been in the position to have them or found the right man to have them with. Rather, the mushy feeling Aiden stirred inside her was more one of kinship. She recalled being a child, not quite as young as he was now, and being worried. What would become of him if something happened to his mother?

No, don't go there. So far, Ginny is doing fine. Travis convinced her to enter a rehab center yesterday. She'll do the work. She has to. For Aiden.

"Thank you for allowing him to hang out here with me."

"It's fine," Mary said, sitting down on the edge of a rocking chair. She seemed mesmerized by the child. "It seems you've gotten close in a short time."

"Me and Aiden? He's a good kid."

Hope felt the intensity of Mary's gaze now focused on her. "I was referring to his uncle. You've met him for dinner, travelled to Buffalo, and now you're babysitting his nephew."

Hope felt her cheeks heat, as if she was being judged. "Yeah, well, but…I'm just helping them out. His mother is…" She glanced at Aiden who was asleep, but still mouthed the word *sick* out of respect for the kid.

"And how is your friend in Buffalo?" Mary asked. Hope had confided in her about Miss June. Mary also knew Hope had come to Hunters Ridge to escape something, but she hadn't pressed for details. Mary was very respectful. Mostly, the Amish woman seemed grateful to have cheap labor, and Hope was happy to have a safe place to live.

"Not well." Hope's voice cracked. "I think she'll be moving into a memory care unit because of her stroke."

"I'm sorry. I'll keep her in my prayers."

"Thank you."

"Maybe you can visit again," Mary suggested.

"I'd love to." Hope rubbed her forehead. "But it's too much of a risk."

"Risk?" The intensity of Mary's gaze unnerved her. "Are you afraid of something?"

"You know that boyfriend I broke up with? He was abusive." Simply saying the words out loud sent a chill coursing across her skin. It was an act of betrayal against her ex.

"Oh dear." Mary's brow furrowed. "Travis is a sheriff's deputy. Can't he do something about him? Arrest him?"

Hope sighed heavily. "That's not how it works." She cleared her throat and her pulse whooshed in her ears. "My ex was a cop, too." She kept her voice low so Aiden wouldn't overhear.

"Oh." The pain and confusion in sweet Mary's eyes touched Hope's heart.

"Being in law enforcement doesn't automatically make someone a good guy. Derek was as mean as they come."

"I'm glad you found your way here." Mary averted her gaze and a pink touched her cheeks.

"Me, too." When Hope made plans for her escape, she felt compelled to return to Hunters Ridge after finding the photo of Mary, her mother, and herself among her mother's things. She had thought the photo held more significance, but maybe its only purpose was to remind Hope of a happier time. Of a nice trip with her mom before she got too ill to travel. "I had no idea how sick my mom was when we took this trip," Hope said, lost a bit in a memory.

If Hope hadn't been watching Mary, she might have missed the subtle wince. Perhaps talking about her mother's death touched too close to home. Mary, after all, was a widow.

"Losing someone is hard. I wasn't sure what I was going to do when Jonah died."

"You've created a nice business here," Hope said. "You should be proud of yourself.

"Proud? No. My Amish neighbors rallied behind me. I couldn't have done it without their support."

"You're lucky. I felt so alone when my mom died," Hope said. "I wish I had family."

"Sometimes you have to make your own family." Mary's eyes traveled to the sleeping child. "You're doing a wonderful thing for him."

"He's had a tough go of it."

"And Miss June is like family, right? She's a good person?" There was something in Mary's tone that made Hope pause, like Mary needed reassurance that Hope's childhood had been a good one despite her mother's untimely death.

"Miss June is a wonderful person." Hope smiled tightly. "It makes me sad that I can't stay by her side because of my old boyfriend."

"You should ask Travis for help," Mary suggested.

Hope shrugged. "I don't know what he could do. Derek is sneaky and knows how to push it just far enough to avoid arrest." She sighed heavily. "His fellow officers support him because they believe his lies."

"You can't run forever," Mary said.

"I suppose not," she said unenthusiastically. But she couldn't face her past until she knew she could fully trust Travis. Maybe then she'd ask him for help.

CHAPTER 14

A few days later Travis had to work overtime after second shift, so Hope kindly offered to babysit Aiden at his house so his nephew could sleep in his own bed. Ginny had been moved to an in-house treatment center and Kerry was still in jail because he couldn't afford bail. And Travis wasn't about to provide him with it.

Shortly after two a.m., Travis texted Hope to let her know he was on his way home. He didn't know how much longer he could take advantage of Hope's kindness, but he hadn't come up with a better solution for his nephew. And Aiden really liked Hope. The boy was coming out of his shell. Travis ran his hand over his hair and slowed at the stop sign. No one was on the road this late. Or early, depending how a person looked at things. Hopefully Ginny would get well soon, and she and Aiden would be reunited. But that wouldn't happen overnight.

Travis glanced down at his phone. Hope hadn't responded to his text. She was probably sleeping. He tossed it back down on the passenger seat of his truck. Was this what it was like to be in a relationship? To let someone know he was done with work and was on his way home? He smiled at the thought. A few bricks fell from the fortress he had built around his heart to protect him from ever having to experience one of those volatile relationships he had witnessed growing up. No good ever seemed to come from that.

The closer he got to his house, the more something niggled at the base of his brain. He forced himself to dismiss it. He convinced himself that she had dozed off. That was all.

When he turned onto his country road, his headlights swept over the reflective lights on the back of a pickup truck parked across the street from his house. He pulled up behind it and made note of the license plate. He got out of the vehicle, walked up to the passenger side and tapped on the window.

"Yeah," the man said.

"Can I help you?" Travis asked.

"I'm lost." The man chuckled, but it sounded forced.

Who just happened to be lost in the middle of the night on a random road? People had GPS nowadays. No reason to pull over. Unless... Travis tracked the man's line of sight. He had a direct view of his house. The only light was the flicker from the television. He turned back around and tilted his head, studying the man. Bald, sagging jowls, disinterested look. Was it someone he had arrested in the past? He had done his best to keep his address private, but it wouldn't take much in a small town for someone to figure out where he lived.

"Tell me where you're going. I can give you directions."

The man started up the vehicle. "No, I'll be on my way."

"Hold up," Travis said, "what's your name?"

The man put his truck into gear and the tires spit out gravel as the vehicle gained purchase and sped away.

Travis jogged back to his vehicle. He had no grounds to

give chase, so he pulled into his driveway. He was relieved to find the front door locked. Inside, Hope was asleep on the couch as he'd suspected. He made a quick check of Aiden asleep in the guest bedroom. All seemed right with the world.

Before waking Hope, he called the station and asked them to run the plate of the suspicious vehicle. He ended the call and turned around to find Hope standing there, rubbing the sleep from her eyes.

She squinted against the light he had turned on over the sink. "What's wrong?"

"How much of that phone call did you hear?" he asked. She glared at him and he figured he owed her the truth. "Some guy was parked out front."

"When?" Fear flashed across her features. "Now?" She rushed to the front window and peered out.

"No, no. He's gone. The guy claimed he was lost."

"Did you get his name?" She seemed to swallow her panic.

"Someone is going to call me back after they run his plates through the system." He took her gently by the elbow and sat her down. "You don't look well. Is there a reason someone would be sitting outside my house?"

"We were so careful," she said with a distant look in her eyes.

"When were we careful? Talk to me." He studied her face, terror etched in the tiny lines around her eyes.

Of course, that makes sense. Why would someone like Hope just show up in Hunters Ridge of all places, and stay?

Sitting on the couch next to him, Hope wrapped her arms tightly around her middle. "I should have never visited Miss June." Her voice shook.

"Tell me what's going on." Travis's tone had a mix of concern and impatience.

"Did you notice anyone following us home from Buffalo

the other day?" Her chest heaved, as if she had run a long-distance race. Or more likely, she was having a panic attack.

He touched her arm and he was surprised when she didn't pull away. Something sparked in her eyes and disappeared. She opened her mouth, then clamped it shut.

"You can trust me."

His phone rang. The sheriff's department ID flashed on the screen. "Let me get this." He answered the phone on speaker.

"I ran the plates," the deputy on duty said. "They belong to a Gerald Gorski. Clean record."

Hope sagged into the couch and covered her face with her hands.

"Thanks, Jake." He ended the call and looked at Hope. "Who is this guy?"

"He's good friends with my ex."

"Is that why you're in Hunters Ridge? You're hiding from an ex?" He studied her face.

Hope drew in a deep breath and the light glistened in her watery eyes. "He's never going to let me go."

Hope's chest felt heavy, making it difficult to breathe. She thought she might puke. She should have never gone to see Miss June. She'd led one of Derek's lackeys right back to her. Someone he paid off to watch for her probably got Travis's license plate from the rehabilitation center's parking lot. The watchful woman on Miss June's floor. She had to be the one.

Stupid. Stupid. Stupid.

"Come on," Travis said calmly. His gentle touch on her arm provided more comfort than he'd understand. She thought Derek had destroyed that for her because she had grown to dread his touch.

She let out a long, slow breath between tight lips. "I'm sorry I'm a mess." Cujo woke up from his spot on the doggy bed in the corner and climbed up on the couch and put his snout in her lap. She took comfort in the little guy's presence. Maybe when she got settled again—wherever that was—she'd get a dog. They made fantastic company.

"You're under a lot of pressure." Travis shifted to the edge of the couch. "Want tea? Water?"

Hope shook her head. She felt drained. Defeated. Defenseless. Tears prickled the back of her eyes. She was vaguely aware of the faucet running in the kitchen and Travis returning to hand her a glass. She took a sip, lost in a recurring nightmare. The cool water slid down her throat, grounding her into the moment.

She set the glass down on the coffee table in front of her. "I have to go." The urgency to flee was strong, but her feet felt leaden, the same feeling she got when she had a to-do list a mile long, was caffeinated, yet felt too jittery and distracted to make any headway. She patted the couch cushions on either side of her, then stuffed her hand down the crease searching for her cell phone. *Nothing.* Little Amos had told her to call anytime, that he'd pick her up. She had to call him. It was too late to even consider trudging through the woods.

Where is my phone?

"You don't have to go," Travis said calmly. Of course *he* was calm. He didn't understand how violent Derek could be.

Oh, where would she go next? How would she make money? A new wave of nausea hit her as she struggled to imagine starting over. Again. What made it worse was that she liked Hunters Ridge and the people she had met.

The adrenaline pumping through her veins gave her a headache behind her eyes. Why had she allowed herself to become fond of Travis and this sweet child? She had only recently met them, but something about them felt like home.

Again, you're making up stories in your mind. A counselor she had met during her years in foster care had told her it wasn't unusual for foster kids to make up stories for reassurance. They cushioned the blow of life's realities.

But no story was going to get her away from her current harsh reality.

"Hope, listen to me. You're safe here."

"No, no…" A band tightened around her lungs and made it difficult to breathe. "Derek is ruthless. He won't stop. He knows I'm here."

The puppy lifted his head, cocked it to one side, then jumped off the couch and curled up in his bed. Apparently he wasn't having any of this either.

Travis tilted his head and paused, seemingly waiting for her to look up at him. When she did, his gaze was warm and reassuring. Was she too easy to trust? What did she know about this man?

"You don't have to run. I'll protect you."

"You can't protect me." Her voice cracked over the words. *I'm the only one who can protect me.*

"I'm a sheriff's deputy. It's my job."

Hope sighed. "Derek is a cop. And he has a lot of friends. It's not as easy as you'd think."

Travis rolled back on his heels and jammed a hand through his hair. "A cop? He's the worst kind of cop." A muscle twitched in his jaw. "The worst kind of man."

Hope twisted her hair up into a ponytail. A nervous habit. She needed to do something with her hands. "I have to go. I'll never be safe in Hunters Ridge. Not anymore."

Travis took her hand in his and looked her directly in the eye. "Don't go."

"I don't trust myself to make good decisions when it comes to men." She sniffed. "I met Derek when I was eighteen. I was naive and he took advantage of me." She focused on Travis's gentle stroke of his thumb across the back of her hand. "He put a wedge between me and Miss June. I was reliant on him for money." She lifted her shoulders, then let them drop. "I felt helpless."

"You're a brave woman," Travis said. The sympathy in his voice almost made her break down.

"I don't know about that, but I couldn't take it anymore. He nearly broke me." She let out a long breath, trying to fight back the emotions bombarding her. "I had to get out before he killed me." She looked up and a tear spilled down her cheek. "I have to go. Derek might do something to you or Aiden. I can't…" Her thoughts were jumbled.

Hope found her purse on the floor by the couch. She picked it up and snagged her cell phone. She fumbled with it, searching for Little Amos's phone number. He could take her back to the B&B to pack what little she had, and then she'd have him take her to the bus depot in Jamestown. This way Travis could stay with Aiden. Yes, yes, that was what she'd do. She stuffed her feet into her shoes while tapping away at her phone screen.

Travis reached out and brushed the back of her hand. Not grabbed. Not yanked. Not slapped. Touched, featherlight, apparently so as not to spook her. "Hope…" Travis seemed to struggle between being assertive and scaring her away. It was a fine line.

The single word. *Hope.* Her fake name made her look up at him. Her nose tingled with all the tears she was fighting back. "I have to go," she whispered. "I'm sorry."

"Where are you going?"

Both Travis and Hope turned their attention to the little boy standing in the hallway. He had his stuffed animal pressed to his face.

"Umm…" Her mind raced. This child had suffered enough trauma due to his drug-addicted parents. She didn't want to add to his worries. "Your uncle is home." She crouched down in front of him and ran her hand over his soft hair. "It's time for me to go home."

"Are you going to babysit me tomorrow?" Aiden asked innocently. "We need to watch that movie you promised."

"Dude, you fell asleep. I watched it tonight." She smiled at him, trying to lighten the mood.

His mouth twitched. "I didn't mean to. I want to see the end of the movie." A hint of alarm threaded his voice. He looked from Hope to his uncle and back.

Travis stepped forward and cupped his nephew's cheek. "It's late. We can watch it tomorrow. I'm off for the next few days." Travis's gaze connected with hers. "I'll be home. Okay?"

The boy nodded, but the expression on his face suggested he wasn't entirely convinced.

"Now why don't you go hop back into bed? I'll be in shortly to tuck you in," Travis said.

Yawning, Aiden walked like a drunken sailor, bumping his shoulder into the wall. When he reached the hallway leading to the bedrooms, he turned. "Can you watch the movie with us?"

Hope stopped tying her shoe and looked up. "Oh, I..." What was she going to say? *I can't stay. I won't stay. It's too dangerous.* She couldn't say any of this to a kid. The world had already been too dark during his five short years on this planet to add any more worries to his little shoulders.

Travis mouthed the words *Please stay.*

Shoving aside her fears, she nodded. *What are you doing?* "Yes, I'll come over to watch the movie tomorrow."

CHAPTER 15

*A*fter Aiden was back in his bedroom, Travis turned to Hope. "I'd prefer if you stayed here."

"I shouldn't…" Hope's response seemed to be automatic. "What will the neighbors say?"

"Forget about the neighbors."

Hope nodded.

"Okay. Let me check on Aiden, then we should talk. *Please.*" After he made sure his nephew was settled, he brought out a large T-shirt and sweatpants for Hope. He found her peering out the window. "Anything out there?"

Hope shook her head. "Not that I can see."

She turned to face him and he held out the oversized T-shirt and sweatpants. "Something more comfortable to sleep in. The clothes will be too big, but the sweatpants have a drawstring in them. They'll probably work, right?"

"Thanks." She accepted the clothes and their hands brushed in the exchange. Their gazes lingered a beat too long.

He took a step backward. "Um, the bathroom is there," he

added awkwardly, pointing to the door down the hallway. "If you need anything else, just holler."

"Thanks. I should probably leave a message for Mary. She'll be worried about me."

"I can send one of the deputies to tell her." Most of the Amish didn't have phones.

"She has a business line for the B&B. I'll leave a message, but at least she'll know I'm not dead in some back alley." It had been an attempt at humor, but based on her crimson face, they both knew it fell flat.

"Does Mary know about your situation?" he asked, keeping his voice low so as not to disturb Aiden.

Hope laughed, a mirthless sound. "My situation." She repeated his choice of words, seemingly considering them. "She knows some things. For one, she had to agree to pay me under the table because I couldn't give her my social security number. Just recently, I told her I was running from my ex who also happens to be a cop."

Travis appreciated that she was willing to share this information with him, but he wondered if she would have ever come clean if he hadn't stumbled upon the man watching the house. He didn't fault her. She was frightened and she had no way of knowing if he could be trusted, no matter what he said. Words were cheap. His father taught him that lesson.

"Why don't you get changed and we'll talk a bit," he suggested. "I'm sure neither of us is going to sleep much tonight." It had to be getting close to three in the morning.

"I haven't slept well in ages." She blinked slowly at him. She seemed to be revealing more and more of herself, little by little.

"I'm sorry you've had to deal with this." He thought of the turmoil his sister had gone through and how she had turned to drugs to dull the pain.

Hope waved her hand in dismissal. She seemed good at deflecting. She turned to go into the bathroom.

"There are new toothbrushes second drawer down," he added, almost relieved to change the subject to something mundane.

She turned and half her mouth cocked into a grin. "Extra toothbrushes, huh?"

He shook his head. "It's not what you're thinking. Well, not what I think you're thinking." It wasn't as if he didn't have the occasional date, some girls he saw a few times, but never a relationship that lasted long enough to invite them to stay in his home and offer them one of his extra toothbrushes. And it wasn't that he was especially old-fashioned, he'd just never found someone he cared to spend that much time with. He liked his space. Having a sleepover meant entertaining a person the next morning. That seemed like too much of a commitment.

A light danced in her eyes. "I'm not thinking anything. I'm happy that I get to brush my teeth." She ran the tip of her tongue across her front top teeth. "They feel like I have moss growing over them." She laughed and closed the door. "Toothpaste in the same drawer?" Her question easily traveled through the thin bathroom door and down the hallway.

"Yep." He smiled.

He took the time to peek in on Aiden again. The child's breath was even. Ah, to sleep the sleep of a child. Travis wondered what he'd need to do to take official custody of the child, even if it was only until his sister got clean. The poor kid deserved a stable home. Consistency.

A few minutes later, Hope joined him on the couch. He had offered her the choice of wine or decaffeinated tea and she had chosen the latter. "I don't drink. Not anymore. Derek ruined that for me. He was the most violent after drinking."

Travis bit back the impulse to repeatedly tell her he was

sorry because he suspected that wasn't what she needed to hear. She needed a plan to move forward without having to hide. She didn't need his sympathy.

"Is Miss June the only family you have back home?" he asked, as if he couldn't wrap his head around the childhood story she had already shared.

"Pretty much. She's been like a grandmother to me after my mom died of cancer."

Travis imagined it was a painful wound. "I'm sorry."

She shrugged but didn't say anything.

"Why did you choose to come to Hunters Ridge? It seems like it'd be easier to get lost in a big city."

"Everything takes money, something I'm short on. I was grateful to find the job with Mary Lapp. One of the first nights after I escaped, I rented a room from her. I think she sensed something was off. We got to talking and she offered me a job." She tilted her head. "I supposed God was looking out for me."

Travis was amazed that the woman oozed gratitude instead of resentment and hate. His respect for her continued to grow.

"How did you get to Hunters Ridge?" He found himself fascinated with Hope's story. There had to be a reason she chose this out of the way place.

"I took a bus to Jamestown, and an Uber from there." She lifted a shoulder. "I couldn't risk asking a friend to drive me here. Derek has a lot of connections." She jerked her thumb toward the front of the house. "As you figured out. Gerald is a retired cop turned private investigator. He's been at my house in Buffalo many times, smoking cigars and laughing it up with my ex." She shook her head, as if lost in a memory. "I can never go back to Buffalo."

Hope stood and crossed the room and grabbed her purse

from the hall table. She came back over and sat down next to him. She reached in and pulled out a photo.

Travis looked at it. Hope leaned over and he could smell her shampoo, and his insides tightened with keen awareness.

"The little girl in the photo is me. That's my mom."

"You're with an Amish woman. Is that Mary Lapp?" He squinted and held the photo a little closer.

"Yes, I thought my mother knew her before, but maybe that was just my perception as a twelve-year-old. That's why I came here. I sensed my mom knew her, but she wouldn't say and I was too young to understand."

"What did Mary have to say about the photo?"

"That she didn't know my mom. That lots of people want to take photos of them even though it's against the *Ordnung*."

"Do you think she's lying?" Travis asked.

"I don't know why she'd lie." Hope bit her bottom lip. She shifted in her seat.

Travis shook his head. "Sometimes people have things to hide."

Hope tugged her long T-shirt down over her hips. "My mom seemed disappointed when we got home, but I never understood why."

Travis returned the photo to Hope. "Your mom was beautiful."

"Thank you." That familiar longing expanded in her chest and made it hard to breathe. She tucked the photo safely away. "My mom died the next winter. Maybe I made up all these stories in my mind. Grasping at straws."

"Sometimes you have to go with your gut."

"In this case, my gut was wrong. Mary has been so nice to me, but she claims to have no memory of that photo." She met Travis's eyes. "Since I'm coming clean." She smiled tightly.

"What is it?"

"My name isn't Hope Baker. It's Harper Miller. I couldn't risk Derek tracking me down by my given name."

Travis reached out and brushed his thumb across her cheek. "Thanks for trusting me, Harper. I will never betray that trust."

CHAPTER 16

*H*ope shifted to the edge of the couch and studied the photo under the lamp. She often wondered who had taken it. Behind them an Amish toddler sat on the grass. That had to be Ada. A pang of nostalgia ached in her heart. Hope missed her mom.

"I'm pretty sure my mom knew she was sick the summer we came here. That's why she made a point of taking this trip with me. I suppose she wanted to create memories. Once I started school, she got sicker. But being twelve, I didn't get it. She slept a lot and got thinner."

"I'm sorry. That must have been horrible to lose your mom at such a young age."

"It was," Hope said, trying not to acknowledge the tears prickling the back of her eyes. "She had been a single mom. That's why I ended up in foster care with Miss June. Miss June never told me, but I'm pretty sure my mom arranged it with her." Hope rarely discussed her upbringing with strangers. One of the few times she did, they took advantage. Derek was able to manipulate and isolate her because she didn't have any other family. And friends didn't stick around once they realized what a jerk Derek was.

"Have you been able to figure out why Hunters Ridge?" Travis asked, snapping her out of her spiraling memories.

She glanced down at the photo again. "No. I heard my mom talking to Mary." She pressed her lips together. "I only recall bits and pieces." She shook her head. "I thought maybe it had to do with my father—who I had never met. But I was young. Maybe I imagined it." Hope sighed heavily. "I wish I had paid more attention back then." It still amazed her that she had gone from age twelve to twenty-five and survived everything she had. The poor little girl in the photo had no idea what was waiting for her in a few short months. She drew in a deep breath then let it out. She stared at the picture one last time before tucking it into her purse between the pages of her novel, something she carried everywhere.

"Would you like help finding your father?" Travis asked around a yawn.

Hope shifted toward the front of the sofa, ready to stand, but she didn't. "You're tired." She tilted her head toward the back hallway. "Your buddy is going to be up early. We can continue this discussion tomorrow."

He shrugged. "I can never sleep in anyway. So, do you want help finding your father?"

Hope sighed. "My father isn't the issue." She turned to look at him. "Derek is. Now that he knows where I am, I'm going to have to leave."

"I'm a sheriff's deputy with a full security system. You're safe here."

"I can't stay holed up here forever."

Travis shook his head. "Just until we can get something on your ex. He needs to be behind bars."

"Derek is too smart. He'll never be punished for what he's done."

"I don't want you to leave, but if you decide that's in your best interest, I'll help you with that, too."

Hope closed her eyes and a warm tear tracked down her cheek. "Will I ever find peace?"

∾

The fine hairs on the back of Hope's neck prickled to life. Her heart raced and her throat went dry. He was here. She could sense him. Feel him. Smell him. Even before he made his presence known. She always could. Her limbs were paralyzed. Maybe if she didn't move, didn't breathe, he'd go away.

"Harp-er," he called, in the familiar singsongy way he did right before his mood turned dark and he accused her of a myriad of things she never did. "Harper!"

The bottom of the mattress tipped with his weight. She kept her eyes squeezed shut. Go away. Go away. Go away. *He never went away. Never, ever... He'd never, ever leave her alone.*

"Where were you tonight?" he asked, his deep voice full of menace.

She tried to open her mouth, but only managed a strangled cry. Sweat slicked her hairline.

"Answer me! Where were you?" The stale smell of bourbon on his breath whispered across her nose. Her stomach revolted but she fought the urge to puke. That would only give him more reason to lash out at her. Call her names.

Again she struggled to answer but couldn't talk. Her lips seemed sealed and her protest came out as a moan. He'd call her weak. Tell her to speak up.

"You sniveling idiot. You think you're going to crawl into bed with that deputy? You think I wouldn't find out about it? he snarled, his hot breath making her cheeks burn. "I'll kill him first. Make you watch. Then I'll take my time with you." The pleasure in his voice came as no surprise to her.

She swallowed around a knot of emotion in her throat.

"You think he might be able to protect himself, but can he protect the boy?"

"You wouldn't hurt a child." The words raced across her mind but got trapped in her throat. *"No!"* The single word exploded through her lips. Finally she had found her voice. *"No! No! No!"*

Hope bolted upright and blinked. The room was pitch-black. Her heart thumped in her ears. Her screams had woken her up from a dream. No, no, a nightmare. Even though it wasn't real, Hope knew Derek wouldn't think twice about hurting Aiden if it meant getting to her.

She flattened her palm against her sweaty neck. She tossed back the comforter and let the cool night air chill her legs. Her mouth was dry.

A soft knock sounded on the door. "Yes?" she called.

The door clicked open and a shadow appeared in the room. *Travis.* His broad shoulders and narrow waist backlit by the dim hallway night-light were unmistakable.

"You okay? I heard shouting."

Hope pulled her bare legs up to her chest and tucked the fabric of his T-shirt under her knees. They couldn't see more than shadows but still… "Sorry. Bad dream."

"You want to talk about it?" Even though Travis respectfully stayed in the doorway, the intimacy of the darkened space and their hushed voices wasn't lost on her.

"No. I'm fine. I'm sorry if I woke you up. I hope I didn't wake Aiden, too."

Travis laughed, and the deep rumble of his voice vibrated through her chest and softened her heart. "He's sprawled out on the bed like he owns the place. And I have a king bed," he added. "He found his way into my room."

"I'm glad *he* can sleep," Hope said softly. "Do you think he'll be able to go home to his mom when she gets better?"

She wasn't sure why she chose now to ask that question. Maybe because his precious nephew's well-being weighed heavily on her mind.

"I hope so. She was clean for a long time before this setback." He sighed heavily and slumped into the doorframe, resting his broad shoulder against it.

"You have your doubts?"

He dragged a hand through his messy hair. "I don't know. After seeing the house, I can't imagine any sober person would live like she and her husband were living." He made a sound of disagreement. "I should have paid closer attention. Ginny has always been good at hiding things. First from my parents, and then, apparently, me."

"How did she make a living?"

"Janitorial services, but she might lose her job after this. Kerry worked construction. She'd say he kept losing jobs because of the economy." The tone of his statement suggested otherwise.

Hope leaned forward and pulled the cover over her legs. "Your nephew is lucky to have you."

"He deserves security and a loving home."

"Take it from me, living in foster care is a tough way to grow up." Hope felt raw and exposed but sharing seemed easier under the cloak of darkness. Travis's shadow shifted and she quickly added, "Sorry I woke you. But I suppose we better get back to sleep. Morning comes quick." She paused a heartbeat, then said, "Night."

"Night, Hope." Travis tilted his head. "Or would you rather I called you Harper?"

She smiled in the darkness, glad that he knew her secret. "Hope. I've come to think of myself as Hope. Besides, it's safer the fewer people know who I really am."

"Okay, sleep well." Travis pulled the door closed.

She listened intently as his bedroom door opened and closed. She imagined him nudging his nephew over a fraction so he could climb back into bed. She focused on the crickets outside the house until she finally drifted off to sleep, praying she wouldn't be met by the boogeyman in her nightmares.

CHAPTER 17

*H*ope woke with a start, unsure of what time it was. Unsure of where she was. For a heartbeat. Then she remembered and a warm and fuzzy feeling embraced her.

Oh boy, she was in trouble. A good kind of trouble for once. But despite her growing feelings for Travis, she still had a huge problem with Derek. He knew where she was.

She rolled over and settled back into her pillows. She'd have to ask Travis where he got them—they were fantastic. Smiling at the thought of Travis, again, she stared at the window trying to guess what time it was. Sunlight poked through the gap between the crooked white roller shade and the wood frame. One thing was certain: it was morning.

I can't stay in bed forever.

Hope flipped back the comforter and climbed out, the wood floor cool on her toes. She yanked open the shade and it snapped back violently onto the roll at the top of the window. "Oops," she muttered, pulling back her hand. Whoever wanted to draw the shade next would have to fight with it.

Outside the window, a tree with vibrant oranges and reds swayed in the wind. The lawn was littered with leaves. Soon the trees would be bare. She squinted, wondering how much Travis could see of the B&B on the adjacent property. It had to be at least a couple football fields that separated the properties. She couldn't help but wonder if she'd still be in Hunters Ridge at that point. Derek was making a case for her to move on—sooner rather than later.

Having lollygagged enough, Hope changed back into her clothes from yesterday and freshened up as best she could. She found Aiden in the kitchen chatting animatedly while his uncle stirred something on the stove.

"After breakfast can we go for a hike in the woods?" Aiden asked.

"Let's eat first and then check the weather." Travis's voice was deep and warm, and Hope had a silly notion of resting her head on his chest to listen to him.

Quietly, she laughed to herself and rolled her eyes. Her apparent weakness for men in law enforcement should have been cured by her horrible experience with Derek.

Travis is not Derek.

"Can Miss Hope come with us?" the little boy asked excitedly.

"I suppose you'll have to ask her when she wakes up."

"She's a sleepyhead," the little boy said, with the slightest of lisps with words starting with S. Funny that she'd never noticed it before. Maybe it came out when he was tired.

"I suppose she is." Travis turned slightly and caught Hope's eye while she lingered in the doorway. "Ah, speak of the devil."

Something about the domestic situation playing out in front of her set her heart aflutter. It shouldn't have to be this way. She was falling for a guy she had no business falling for. No, her jerk of an ex knew where she was, and she refused to bring Aiden and Travis into her mess. Her dream last night wasn't real, but Derek's violence was. All too real. Of course, Travis could handle himself, but Aiden had already witnessed too much disfunction in his life. Another situation would probably make the poor kid believe most men treated people close to them like complete jerks. It would be a heavy burden to bear. For anyone, least of all a five-year-old child. She couldn't put him through this.

"Morning." Hope forced a smile, despite her insides suddenly feeling hollow. Her emotions were all over the place.

Travis reached up and grabbed a mug from the cabinet. He pointed to a Keurig in the corner of the counter. "I have lots of kinds of coffee. What can I get you? Or, if you'd rather, help yourself. I should also have tea bags around here somewhere." He pivoted in place, as if trying to decide where that somewhere would be.

"Coffee would be great. I'll help myself. Thanks." She needed a boost of caffeine. And a shower, but that could wait.

"I can make you some eggs, too, if you'd like," Travis offered.

She lifted a hand. "Do you have bread? I'd much rather have toast."

"Check the bread drawer."

Hope found some wheat bread and popped two pieces into the toaster. Travis slid a plate of eggs in front of Aiden, then excused himself. A few minutes later, Hope heard the shower turn on. She fixed her coffee, then slid into the chair next to Aiden's.

The child leaned over and grabbed the ketchup, flipped the lid off and squeezed. "My dad says ketchup on eggs is gross. But me and my mom love ketchup. On everything."

"I've never tried ketchup on my eggs." And she probably wouldn't be starting today. She felt a little nauseous on an empty stomach, therefore her choice of toast. She figured she'd walk over to the B&B and check in with Mary.

She prayed Derek's goons hadn't figured out where she lived and worked. The entire situation made her so mad, but her anger had never gotten her anywhere. She had to be calm, focused, smart. She couldn't afford to pick up and move every time she suspected Derek was on her heels, but she also couldn't risk that he'd hurt people she cared about.

Her toast popped, startling her back to the moment. She buttered it, then returned to her seat.

Aiden ate a few mouthfuls of egg and chased it down with a sip of orange juice. His face grew red and he said, "I miss Momma." The comment came out of left field, catching Hope off guard.

She had to swallow around her emotion, trying to be the calm he needed. "I know, sweetie. I know."

"Is my mom better?" he asked, looking up at her while his lip quivered.

"She's getting the help she needs to get better." Hopefully, this time rehab would stick.

The little boy seemed to give it some thought, then nodded. He picked up his fork and began eating his eggs again.

A few minutes later, Travis appeared in the doorway with fresh clothes and damp hair. Self-consciously, Hope plucked at her shirt from yesterday.

"Looks like rain *is* moving in." Travis put his mug in the microwave to warm up his coffee.

"Can we still go for a hike?" Aiden asked, clearly concerned that his plans were going to get ruined.

"I suppose we can wear raingear." Travis glanced at Hope, clearly an invitation. "You want to come with?"

Hope hated to refuse Aiden—or Travis—but she feared the more time she spent, the harder her goodbye would be.

She glanced down at her chipped fingernails. "All I have are the clothes on my back." It wasn't exactly an answer.

"I could probably find a raincoat. No doubt you'd drown in it, but it'd keep you dry."

Just then, a loud thunderclap rumbled directly over the house, making her jump. The electric stillness was shattered by heavy raindrops pinging the windowpanes.

Aiden scooted out of his chair and raced to the window. "It's raining a lot." His posture sagged and he backed up and slumped into the couch.

Travis tousled the kid's hair. "Probably too much for a hike. We could play a board game instead?"

Aiden bolted upright. "You have games?"

Travis nodded. "In the closet in the family room. Finish your breakfast, then go pick out your favorite."

After breakfast, Hope found herself snuggled into a blanket next to Travis while Aiden knelt on the other side of the coffee table, poised to kick butt and take names family-game-day style.

After a while, Hope lost track of how many games they had played. She thought back: Chutes and Ladders, Trouble, some special kid-themed Monopoly, and Life. She knew she was missing one or two. They didn't necessarily play all the way through, and they most definitely fudged the rules, allowing Aiden to dictate the pace. Apparently Travis had picked up the games at Goodwill for just such an occasion. Spending her morning playing board games and laughing like she hadn't laughed in ages was exactly what she had needed, too.

The rain continued at a steady pace and Travis made them peanut butter and jelly sandwiches with chips for lunch. After, they decided to watch a family-friendly movie. Hope found herself dozing on and off in between thinking she should really go home. But she couldn't remember the last time she had felt so content.

At some point, Hope had dozed off and woke to Travis's phone buzzing on the coffee table. He gently touched her thigh, as if reassuring her that everything was okay. She sat up straight and heat warmed her cheeks when she realized she had been using his bicep as a pillow. Not nearly as soft as the ones in the guest room, but definitely nice.

She sighed and ran a hand across her face. She had a crick in her neck and she hoped she hadn't drooled on him. She laughed at herself.

"What?" Travis said, seemingly in no hurry to answer the phone.

"Nothing, just thinking I haven't been very good company."

Travis raised an eyebrow and a half-smile slanted his lips. So handsome. "You've been perfect company."

Oh boy...

Aiden sounded out the name on the caller ID. "Bright-er Days."

Travis jolted forward and snagged the phone. "I should get this." Then into the phone he said, "Hello." He stood and ran his hand over his hair, his relaxed, sexy demeanor shifting to all business. "Yes, yes, this is Travis Hart. I'm her brother." He disappeared down the back hall and closed his bedroom door behind him for privacy.

Hope's stomach bottomed out. Something had happened. She scooted forward to pick up some of the scattered game pieces and her neck tweaked. That was what she got for falling asleep on Travis. She watched Aiden who appeared engrossed in some kid movie with talking dogs, thankfully unaware of the shift in mood.

Hope stood and tugged on the thighs of her pants. "I'll be right back, buddy." She wasn't sure when she started calling him by the nickname Travis used. "I'll want you to fill me in on what I missed, okay?"

"You've been sleeping. You missed a lot," he said, keeping his intense gaze on the screen. Cujo lifted his head, then set it back down on the boy's lap.

"True," Hope said distractedly. She glanced out the window, and the day was still dark and gloomy. She should really call Mary and make sure she didn't need her to work. They still had tomorrow to get ready for this weekend's guests.

Hope strolled down the hallway with the blanket from the couch still wrapped around her shoulders. The room wasn't cold, yet a chill raced down her spine. Travis's deep voice rumbled through the door but she couldn't make out the words, nor did she want to. She needed to know what was going on, but she didn't want to eavesdrop.

She knocked quietly, then opened the door without getting an invitation. Travis waved her in and pointed at the door to close it. He was wrapping up the call.

"What is it?" she asked when he hung up. "Everything okay with Ginny?" She said the words so quietly they were little more than a thought.

A muscle worked in Travis's jaw. "She overdosed."

Again?

"Oh no…" Terror sent pinpricks racing up her arms. "How? I don't understand. I thought she was in rehab."

"She got ahold of something." Travis scrubbed a hand over his face and looked around, his eyes filled with worry. "I hate to ask this, but can you stay here with Aiden? They're taking Ginny by ambulance to the hospital. They're not sure she's going to make it"—his voice cracked—"and I need to be there."

Hope's heart sank. She had wanted to get away to avoid bringing trouble to this kind man's doorstep, but how could she tell him no when the worst kind of trouble had already landed in his lap?

He must have noticed her hesitancy because he said, "Of course, I can reach out to a neighbor. I shouldn't have presumed... Wait, you need to stay safe." Like her, he seemed to have a million thoughts swirling through his brain.

"No, no, of course I can stay. Please go. We'll be fine." She refused to add any more drama to this man's plate. A horrible sinking sensation settled in her gut, as if she was trapped.

"Lock the doors and I'll show you how to set the alarm. This place is like a fortress. I promise. I'll have a deputy come sit in the driveway until I get back. I'm sure I can get the sheriff to okay it."

"That's asking a lot of someone. I don't think that's necessary." Of course it might be necessary, but Hope's need to be "no trouble" had been ingrained in her after dating a control freak like Derek.

"I'll be back as soon as I can," he said, almost as if on autopilot.

"Sure." Hope forced a reassuring smile as she placed a hand on his bicep. "I'm really sorry, Travis. I hope she's okay."

They locked gazes for a long moment, then he just gave her a quick nod. "Don't say anything to Aiden. Um, I'll tell him I got called into work."

Hope nodded, unable to speak around the lump of emotion in her throat. She followed him to the family room where he said goodbye to Aiden. The boy barely lifted his eyes from the screen and Hope couldn't help but study him, feeling awful for what he was about to go through.

Hope forced a cheery tone and sat down on the couch. "Looks like you're about to start another movie."

Aiden nodded. To her surprise, the little boy climbed up onto the couch and scooted up against her, resting his head on her shoulder. She patted his knee and found herself saying a silent prayer for his mother. Prayer had been a source of frustration for Hope—God hadn't answered many of her prayers over the years—but she prayed, for this kid's sake, that he didn't lose his mother.

Hope wouldn't wish that kind of loss on anyone.

CHAPTER 18

*H*ope and Aiden watched a couple movies, played cards, and then built a fort with the couch cushions. She was keenly aware of the time ticking by without any word from Travis. She hoped this meant Ginny was on her way to recovery. Because death would have been quick, right? Or maybe Hope was doing a bit of wishful thinking.

Every so often she'd stroll by the window to see that a sheriff's deputy was still sitting in the driveway. She was discreet so as not to alarm Aiden. She felt safe from Derek, but her frustration at not hearing from Travis was wearing on her.

It wasn't until Travis's nephew said he was hungry that she realized how late it had gotten. She found a frozen pizza in the freezer. They settled in to watch even more TV. The little boy didn't seem to mind, but Hope was growing bored.

When she cleared the plates, she looked out the window again. This time, Aiden came up behind her. "Is that Uncle Travis?"

"No, buddy. It's one of his friends."

Aiden frowned. "Why are they here? Did you do something bad?"

"No, nothing like that," Hope said, pulling him against her side. "They're just hanging out there." Even as she said it, she realized how ridiculous she sounded. "Want to see if your uncle has some popcorn? What's movie night without popcorn, right?"

"No thanks," Aiden said politely. "My daddy is in jail." The statement came out matter of fact.

Hope jerked her head back, caught off guard. "I'm sorry to hear that." She decided to take the *play dumb* role.

"Will they let him out if my mommy dies?" Aiden swiped his cheek with a balled fist.

Hope guided him back to the couch. She reached out and gently squeezed the boy's hand. "You have a lot of worries for a little kid."

"I'm not little." Aiden drew in a deep breath and exhaled a world-weary sigh.

"I didn't mean that as a bad thing," Hope said, tilting her head to see his face better.

"My dad tells me to be a man." Aiden pulled his hand out from under hers and ran them down his thighs.

Hope drew in a deep breath, trying to process her thoughts. Why was it that men who didn't know how to be men always demanded it from others? "You're allowed to be a kid, buddy. There's plenty of time, say after you turn eighteen, to be a man." She tried to sound playful, even though anger at his thoughtless father surged through her brain.

"My daddy hurts my mommy. Is that why my mommy is in the hospital?"

Hope's mouth went dry. Poor kid. Both parents had addiction issues, and Travis obviously didn't care for his brother-in-law, but she hadn't heard anything about domestic abuse. Sadly, considering everything else, it didn't surprise her. And as a victim of abuse, she couldn't imagine what it would be like to witness it as a child.

"I'm sorry your dad hurts your mom." She tried to offer him words that she would have liked to hear. "That's wrong. No person deserves to be hurt by another person." How many times did she have to say that over and over to herself before she'd had the courage to get out? Sadly, she realized, even the most courageous women sometimes couldn't escape their abusers.

Aiden shook his head, his big brown eyes wide and fearful. "He said it was an accident. Mommy said he didn't mean it. He loves us so much. We have to be really good so he doesn't get mad no more." He was obviously repeating what he had heard his mother tell him. "We shouldn't make him mad."

A cold, hollow dread pooled in her belly. If she was talking to another adult, she knew what she'd say—that this man was full of it. Derek used to rage about the exact same thing. How *she* had done something wrong and made him lash out. Since Aiden was only five years old and he undoubtedly loved both his mother and father, she had to choose her words carefully.

She closed her eyes and said a silent prayer. *Please, Lord, help me tell him the right thing. Give me wisdom.* The prayer came out of nowhere and she wondered why she chose now to pray.

Lean on your faith when you need it. Her mother's voice whispered across her brain even as Hope's cynicism about the usefulness of prayer reared its head. Her most fervent prayers didn't save her mom.

"Aiden, I know you love your mom and dad—"

"I don't love my dad," he interrupted, speaking more harshly, "because he hits my mom."

"I'm sorry. No one should have to see their daddy hurt

their mommy." She fought to keep her voice from breaking. "Have you ever told anyone?" She understood at this point it probably didn't matter. "Maybe a teacher."

"I don't go to school. I'm supposed to start next time." By next time he must mean next fall.

"You haven't told anyone?" she pressed. "How about your Uncle Travis? He'd help you."

Aiden shook his head. "It's a secret."

"Who told you it was a secret?" The more she learned, the more she despised the man who'd nearly killed her by running into the Wash & Go in a drugged-out haze.

"Momma." His quiet voice made him seem younger than his five years.

"Your mother?" Hope tried to keep the surprise from her tone but undoubtedly failed. Now, why should she be surprised? If Aiden spoke up, it would cause problems for his mom, too. Different problems. "She was probably afraid. Your mother loves you so much. You know that, right?"

Aiden nodded and he seemed on the verge of crying. He didn't fight her comforting embrace. Hope's mind drifted back to all the times she had told her friends that everything was okay between her and Derek. Wasn't that the same thing? She hated to think what would have happened if she didn't get out. If she had brought children into the world with him. She might have felt obligated to stay then. Trapped.

Hope gazed around the room, trying to think of more ways to distract this sweet child. A subtle buzzing sounded somewhere in the room.

"Your phone's making a noise," Aiden said.

Hope stood up and glanced around, trying to remember where she had left it. Her heart jackhammered and a rush of tingles rained down over her. Maybe this was news about Ginny. Or maybe Miss June. Either way, it could be bad. She let out a quick breath between narrowed lips, trying to pull it together. She couldn't fall apart in front of Aiden. She realized the sound was coming from her purse. She dug for it and hit answer even though she didn't recognize the number, surprised that she even got reception.

"Hello there, Harper." Derek's cool voice raked over her.

She froze, unable to move.

"You didn't think I'd find you. Stupid girl."

Her voice squeaked and she fumbled with the phone to hit "end" and tossed it on the couch. Her eyes darted around the room and the adrenaline surging through her veins made it impossible to think clearly.

"Was that Uncle Travis?" Aiden asked.

"Um, no, no it wasn't." Her voice shook and she felt like she was above herself looking down. That was the kind of panic her ex induced.

The phone started vibrating again. Aiden scooped up the phone.

"No, leave it!" Hope shouted, louder than she had intended. Seeing Aiden's shocked response, she quickly added, "It's a telemarketer. That's all." She took the phone from him and stuffed it into her back pocket.

A moment later, she felt the buzz of a text. Her anxiety wouldn't allow it to go unread. She pulled the phone out and glanced at the screen. Her heart nearly exploded. It was a photo of this house. A sheriff's car sitting in the driveway.

Through the rain-spattered window she could see the front end of the patrol car. But from this angle she couldn't see the deputy. She considered going out there and telling him what had transpired, but decided she'd call the station so she wouldn't have to leave the house. With trembling fingers she called 911 and the called dropped. *Ugh.*

She ran to the kitchen and grabbed the portable landline

phone. She reached dispatch of the Hunters Ridge Sheriff's Department almost immediately.

After she explained the situation, the officer said, "Hold on, I'll patch you through to Deputy Lehman. He's the deputy assigned to Travis's house."

After a long stretch, dispatch came back on.

"The deputy is not answering. Can you look out and see if he's there? Perhaps Johnny's walking the perimeter and didn't take his radio. Cell reception is spotty out there."

Hope rushed to the front window and peered out through the side of the curtain. "I can only see the bumper of the patrol car. I can't see the driver's seat."

"I'm going to send another deputy to you. Don't hang up." The dispatcher spoke calmly and professionally.

While holding the phone to her ear, Hope searched outside again. That was when the fringes of her vision went dark and her entire world moved in slow motion. Out by the road a man stood staring at the house, his hair slicked to his head from the rain. *Derek.* Adrenaline surged through her veins and the flight response was strong.

"Oh no," she whispered. "No, no, no, no…"

"What's wrong?"

Hope dropped the corner of the curtain and looked down at Aiden. Her voice cracked as she spoke into the phone. "My ex is out front and"—she carefully chose her words knowing the child was listening—"I believe he wants to hurt me." It broke her heart that he had to witness this. "My ex is the reason there's a deputy stationed outside."

"Ma'am, stay locked in the house. I have another deputy on the way."

Right then, the window exploded. The curtain expanded in a poof, then all the glass rained down behind the thick fabric. Cujo jumped to his feet and started barking, adding to the chaos. He was ready to attack the large rock that sat in

137

the center of the room. The alarm blared, Hope couldn't stand here and wait. She refused to be a victim.

"He broke the window. I can't stay here."

"Ma'am," the dispatcher said, "tell me what's going on."

"We're going out through the back. You'll find us somewhere between here and the bed-and-breakfast on Route 321."

"Ma'am, ma'am," the dispatcher said more urgently, but the time for discussion had passed. Hope hung up and slid the phone into her back pocket.

Cujo jumped around at their feet and nearly took out Hope's legs. She bent down and clutched Aiden's shoulders. The poor kid had his hands pressed against his ears from the horrible screeching of the alarm. "Get your shoes on. Now."

"Where are we going?" he hollered.

"Quick, we don't have time. We're going to go to my house through the woods."

"At night?" Excitement lit his eyes, as he tentatively pulled his hands away from his ears.

"Let's go." They ran to the back mudroom and got their shoes on. Their sneakers wouldn't be a match for the rainy woods, but they didn't have much choice. Cujo jumped up on her calf and barked, determined to be included on their outing.

Hope knew she'd never be able to keep the dog quiet, she just prayed the strident alarm would mask his barks.

"Aiden, we're going to race, okay? Across the backyard and into the woods."

He nodded with the intensity of a little kid who had run similar drills. Had his mother held his hand, urging him to be quiet so his father wouldn't hear him? The thought broke her heart.

"Wait here." She ran back and peered out through a different window facing the street. Derek was nowhere to be found, but his truck was out there. "Oh no, no, no," she whispered. *Where are you?*

Without wasting another moment, she rushed back to Aiden, snagging her cell phone on the way. Darn thing was probably going to be useless out there. Without turning off the alarm, she unlocked the back door.

With Cujo's leash in one hand and the child's hand in the other, she said, "Let's go."

CHAPTER 19

Travis held his sister's delicate hand while she lay unconscious, her thin frame a small lump under the white hospital blankets. His mind wouldn't shut down. When he wasn't begging God to spare her, he was angry about all the horrible choices his sister had made that landed her here. The doctors hadn't given him much hope for his sister's recovery. Her organs were shutting down. But an elderly aunt once told him, "Where there's life, there's hope." So he bowed his head and prayed a little harder.

When he wasn't scared for his sister, he was worried about his nephew and Hope. He was wound so tight every muscle in his body ached. He drew in a deep breath and released it, reminding himself that a fellow deputy was sitting in his driveway making sure they were safe.

Travis glanced up at the analog clock on the wall. His mother had said she'd be here hours ago. It wouldn't be entirely uncharacteristic for her not to show up. A new wave of anger washed over him as he replayed the conversation with his mother in his head. As it was, when Travis told her the horrible news, his mother had questioned its veracity. It didn't fit her narrative as a reformed drug user turned wonderful mother. She might have given up drugs, but she also never made it up to the children she ruined.

"After all, your sister tends toward the dramatic," she had said nonchalantly, as if he had called about a broken arm or a few stitches.

Travis wasn't sure if this denial was out of self-preservation or a fear of looking bad in the eyes of her church.

His mother's booming voice reached the hospital room before she did, as if conjured out of his thoughts. "I'm sure she'll be fine," his mother said to someone in the hallway. "She always is."

"Right this way, Mrs. Hart," another woman responded, most likely a nurse who was probably wondering if someone hadn't updated this poor woman on the gravity of her daughter's situation.

His mother appeared in the doorway dressed in a beige ankle-length raincoat, her arms full. Travis stood and rushed to his mother, taking the items—magazines, a makeup bag, and a plastic container with chocolate chip cookies. His mother obviously had ignored everything he had said.

She fussed with finding a spot for her coat before settling on draping it over the back of the vinyl chair. She finally turned to look at her daughter. Really look at her. All the color drained from his mother's face and her posture sagged. Travis grabbed one side of her while the nurse grabbed the other.

"Mother, sit here." Travis ushered her to the chair he had just vacated. He nodded his thanks to the nurse. "I got her."

"Are you sure?" the nurse asked.

"Yes, thank you." Travis gave her a tight smile.

"What happened?" His mother stared at her only daughter. "She looks *so* sick."

Travis would have laughed if it wasn't so sad. Ginny and

his mother had been estranged for years. Ginny blamed her mother for her addiction, and her mother couldn't understand why Ginny couldn't conquer her demons when she herself had been sober for over a decade.

"She overdosed. A second time. She entered rehab, then while there she got access to drugs." Travis wrapped his hands around the footrail.

His mother turned her tear-stained face toward him. "But she'll be okay. She's overdosed before and she was just fine."

Just fine was an overstatement, but Travis suspected he knew what his mother meant. "She lost too much oxygen to her brain."

His mother lifted a shaky hand and scratched her head. "I don't understand."

"There's nothing more they can do. It's a matter of time." He had to fight to keep his voice from breaking. He had to be strong for his mother.

"No, no, no..." His mother bowed her head, resting it on her daughter's hand. Her pitiful wails were muffled in the bedding. After a moment, she looked up, her face all splotchy from crying. "Does Kerry know?"

"He's still in jail." As far as Travis was concerned, he could rot there.

"Can't you do something about that?" she asked.

"Why? He's done nothing for Ginny."

"Virginia," his mother corrected.

"He's partially responsible for this..." He stared at his sister's face. She had a strange greenish-yellow color with dark rings under her eyes. *Ginny, why?* He let out a frustrated breath. "He'll have to live with his guilt. I'm not going to pull any strings to get him out."

His mother pursed her lips and seemed to shudder. Was she reflecting on her own negative influence over her daughter's life? Travis hated to be so heartless, but he was furious.

His big sister was going to die. His nephew was going to lose his mother. He sighed and placed his hand on his mother's shoulders; that was all the compassion he could muster without falling apart himself. The blinking lights on the machines monitoring his sister's vitals scraped across his nerves as he struggled to manage his emotions.

How would he ever break the news to Aiden?

CHAPTER 20

*H*ope held Aiden's hand in one of hers and the dog leash in the other as they bolted across the backyard. The wind rustled the leaves, and clouds raced across the sky. The rain had stopped, but the grass soaked through her sneakers. The sound of crickets filled the night air, and somewhere in the distance an owl hooted. Every detail seemed exaggerated. Every muscle was taut as she braced herself expecting Derek to lunge out from the darkness and take her down by her hair.

The wailing of the house alarm faded as they approached the tree line. "Aiden," she said, not slowing her pace, "no matter what happens, keep running."

The moonlight caught the fear in his eyes and she hated that she was responsible for doing this to him. She squeezed his hand reassuringly as they moved deeper into the woods.

Cujo tugged her arm in the opposite direction, surprising her with his strength. He was such a happy, goofy dog, sniffing every tree, bush and blade of grass. She yanked on his leash, then realized he was trying to do his business. "Come on, buddy," she muttered. As soon as he was finished, she squatted down and scooped him up, grunting at the weight of him.

"Didn't Uncle Travis tell us to stay inside?" Aiden asked as she lumbered under the weight of the dog in one arm as she pulled the little boy along in the other.

"My job is to protect you," she said breathlessly. She glanced over her shoulder, wondering if she'd see Derek if he came into the heavily shadowed backyard.

"From that bad man?"

"Yes," she whispered, "we need to be quiet." *Please, God, let this be the right decision.*

Hope kept moving forward, not stopping, despite the sharp ache in her side. She wished she was familiar with the property so she could find the shortest route between his house and Mary's B&B without getting caught up in the underbrush.

Fallen tree branches snapped under their feet. Low branches whacked their vinyl jackets and Cujo let out a loud bark. Hope bowed her head and pressed her cheek against the top of his head. "It's okay. We'll get you treats soon."

As they got deeper into the woods, Hope slowed, gasping huge breaths of air.

"Man, I'm out of shape," she whispered. She finally had to set Cujo down, making sure to wind the leash tightly around her hand, fearful he'd dart after some nocturnal animal. She didn't want Aiden's precious dog to go missing along with everything else. "Are you okay?" she asked Aiden. Her eyes were slowly adjusting to the dark.

"I ripped my jacket," he said, pressing his hand to his belly. "My mom's going to be mad."

"Don't worry." She stared back in the direction they came, trying hard to focus on what he was saying.

A strange light flowed over Travis's house. She narrowed

her gaze, finally realizing that it must be from the high beams of Derek's truck.

"We have to keep going." She turned back around and the forest looked like a wall of black. A wave of panic sent a sheen of sweat prickling her hairline.

Perhaps Aiden had better night vision than she had, but he somehow managed to weave them through the woods, despite their shoes slipping and sliding in the mud and wet leaves. Suddenly, the sound of her breathing was broken by a harsh yelling on the wind.

"Har-per! Har-per!" Derek screamed. "I'm going to find you."

Her heart leapt out of her chest and she bit back a yelp. Thankfully, Aiden kept moving, perhaps not aware that the shouting was directed at her. He knew her as Hope.

After another five minutes they stepped out of the trees and into a field. Hope recognized the back of the barn on the Lapps' property. She loosened her death grip on Cujo's leash and shook out her numb hand. The dog sniffed happily and lifted his leg on the nearest tree.

"Come on," Hope said, glancing over her shoulder. "Let's get inside and call your uncle."

Hope's knees began to tremble. It was the first time she allowed herself to feel—*really* feel—the emotions rolling over her. Maybe Derek had done something to the deputy. She thought of the young man who had introduced himself when he arrived. He had assured her she'd be safe under his watch.

Please let him be okay.

If he wasn't, it would be all her fault.

Travis couldn't sit still one more minute watching his mother's lips move as she recited prayers over her daughter's failing body. The prayer might have been one of the "please don't take my child" type pleas or a more formal "let Thy will be done" prayer. Travis never risked one of the latter prayers because he didn't trust God to not strike him down for pretending he was worthy of answered prayers.

Travis stared at the top of his mother's head; her white part having grown out. He had shown up once at her apartment while she was coloring her hair a jet black that made her look older than she was. She had always been vain that way. Always. She worried about her appearance even when her strange actions—fueled by drugs and alcohol—made her the subject of the rumor mill. She never seemed to get the irony. Travis ran his hand over his hair and sighed, frustrated with how much resentment he still harbored toward his mother despite her decade-long sobriety.

Shaking his head, he let his gaze drift to his sister's face. She was a shell of the woman she had been when she was clean. That same time in her life coincided with her separation from Derek. When he reentered her life, so did the drugs. A knot twisted in his gut. He had a hard time wrapping his head around the situation. Ginny had overdosed. He had saved her, giving her a second chance. Then she overdosed again.

Maybe she didn't want to be saved, a voice in his head taunted him.

His heart ached for his sister, but more so for Aiden. Ginny made choices. The poor kid did nothing to deserve this.

The incessant beeping of the machines keeping her alive began to make his nerves buzz. He pulled out his phone and clicked the music app. He chose a station that he hoped his sister would like and set his phone down on the bedside table. The music filled the otherwise sterile room, softening the hard edges. He met his mother's gaze and she nodded her approval. Strange, because it wasn't often he and his mother agreed on things.

Urgent footsteps grew closer, forcing him to look up. Deputy Caitlin Flagler appeared in the doorway and she gestured toward him. The look on her face sent another surge of panic slicing through him. With his heart racing in his ears, he touched his mother's shoulder as he walked past. "I'll be right back."

He stepped into the hallway.

"What is it?" He had been trained to respond to emergencies, but the energy felt off. He might need to take time away from his job to get his sense of equilibrium back. A spooked sheriff's deputy could get people killed. He found himself looking back at his mother still bent in prayer over his dying sister.

Things will never be normal again.

"You need to come with me," Caitlin said.

Prickles rained down over Travis's scalp. "Talk to me. What's going on?"

"Let's walk and talk." The deputy pointed with her chin in the direction of the red *Exit* sign. They strode down the hospital corridor. "There's been an incident at your house."

"What kind of incident?" Travis paused, his stomach dropping.

"Come on," the deputy urged. "We need to get you there. We'll talk in the car."

Travis snapped into emergency response mode. "My nephew and Hope Baker are there. Has anyone talked to them?"

"No, the tactical response team hasn't been able to get anyone on the phone."

"Tactical response?" He shot one last glance in the direction of his sister's room. She was dying. He needed to be there for her.

He blinked. Her son was in danger. Ginny would want him to focus on her child.

"Lead the way," he said with a confidence he didn't feel. His entire world was shifting beneath him.

The other deputy walked ahead of him as they jogged down the stairs, then out through the automatic doors to the parking lot. A patrol car was parked by the curb and they both hopped in. Caitlin put the vehicle into drive and sped out of the parking lot.

She held out her hand toward him but kept her eyes on the road. "First, you need to know that Johnny is in surgery."

A rock weighed on Travis's chest and he could hardly breathe. "Deputy Lehman? What happened?" Johnny was a rookie deputy.

"He was ambushed. Shot."

"And Hope and Aiden?"

"We haven't been able to contact them. Does she have a cell phone you could call?"

"Yes, yes…" Travis patted his pockets and muttered under his breath. "I don't have my phone. I left it at my sister's bedside." His thoughts were scattered. "And Johnny. Is he going to be okay?"

"They'll know more after surgery."

Travis plowed a hand through his hair and cursed under his breath. The engine on the patrol car whirred, racing toward his house. He snagged the handset to the police radio. "Dispatch, this is Deputy Travis Hart. Put me through to whoever's on the scene at my house."

"Yes, sir."

Travis wasn't surprised when Sheriff Lyle Fitzgerald— "Fitz"—answered the call. He was new on the job after Sheriff Littlefield had gotten caught up with some extremists last winter. The mayor had decided they needed to bring in someone from outside. Someone objective, untainted by local scandal. Fresh blood.

Travis shoved all his emotions down. "Sir, what's the situation?"

"Deputy Lehman was approached from behind and shot when he was checking the perimeter. He was found after a passerby saw a commotion. Your front window is smashed. Someone threw something through it."

"Did they catch the guy?"

"No, but there's a black pickup registered to a Derek Wall parked on your lawn."

Travis swallowed hard. "Wall is a cop in the Buffalo area. He has been stalking a friend of mine, Hope Baker." He made an instantaneous decision to go with her assumed name, not sure how this whole thing would play out. "Hope is babysitting my five-year-old nephew, Aiden, at my house." A pounding started behind his eyes. "Any sign of them yet?"

"No sign of either the woman or the child. We do have a lone gunman taking shots at our deputies. He's set up in your house."

Travis shoved aside the thought of someone invading his personal space and focused on the immediate concern. "Anyone else hurt?"

"No." Some commotion sounded over the radio. "You know this guy? Any chance you could talk him out?"

"I don't think I'm the guy. If anything, he'd want to put a bullet in my head for helping his ex hide."

Travis closed his eyes briefly, then looked out the windshield. The middle white line on the road rushed past, but not fast enough. He checked a mile marker on the side of the road.

"I'm five minutes out," Travis said. "I'm willing to try to talk to him. Maybe he's mad enough at me to make a mistake and let us get him."

"It's worth a shot," the sheriff said.

"One we have to take." Travis didn't want to verbalize what the worst case might be. They were all professionals here. They had seen worst-case.

Straight ahead of him his quiet country house was awash in light. Now would be a good time to commit a crime across town because one hundred percent of the patrol cars were parked on the road and in fields surrounding his property.

The deputy hadn't even engaged the brake when Travis opened the door. She slammed on the brake and he climbed out. He ran over to the sheriff. Another deputy nearby had a sniper's rifle trained on his house.

"Have you made contact?" Travis's gaze jumped from dark window to dark window of his house.

The sheriff tipped his chin toward the left window. The room where he watched TV. "Saw slight movement ten minutes ago. Nothing since."

Travis tapped the trunk of the sheriff's patrol car. "Give me your rifle. I'll go down the street a bit, then circle around. Take him by surprise around the back of the house." He was not going to let this jerk hurt his nephew or Hope. He should have never left them alone. He'd never forgive himself if something happened to them. Aiden was just a kid. And Hope... He wanted time to get to know her better. He was finally opening his heart...

The sheriff nodded his agreement, then pointed at a few other deputies to give them orders. "Go with Deputy Hart."

Travis shook his head. "I'm going alone. I don't want to draw his attention away from all the patrol cars out front. Everyone stay put."

The sheriff stared at him for a heartbeat, then gave a terse nod. "Be safe."

CHAPTER 21

A bead of sweat dripped down Hope's face as she quickly ushered Aiden inside the B&B.

"I want Uncle Travis," he said as she turned around and locked the door.

"We'll get him. Don't worry."

Mary had said the locks were added after she turned this place into a B&B. Apparently *Englischers*, as she called them, were less trusting of outsiders than the Amish, who often didn't have locks on their doors. *Strange.*

Instinctively, Hope reached out and cupped the precious boy's cheek. He was flushed from the exertion and the chilly night air. "I'll call your uncle." The landline was in the barn because it would have been pushing the limits to have it inside the house. She dug out her cell phone from her thick winter coat and checked it again. No bars. It was amazing anyone out here ever got someone on the phone. Reception was spotty and unpredictable.

She helped Aiden unzip his coat so he wouldn't overheat. She slung it over the back of the chair. She noticed a few pieces of paper with Mary's handwriting, then remembered the B&B would be expecting guests tomorrow evening. A whisper of guilt niggled at her. Mary had been kind to her and Hope hadn't been fulfilling her end of the deal this week. She slipped out of her coat and placed it over Aiden's.

"Hello there." Mary appeared in the doorway, a white gown under a black robe. Cujo ran over to the woman and jumped up on her.

"Off," Hope said and the dog complied.

"He's fine." Perhaps reading something in Hope's expression Mary added, "What's going on? Is everything okay?"

Hope met her friend's gaze and slowly nodded, not wanting to say too much in front of the child. She placed her hand on Aiden's back. "You must be tired. You can rest on the couch."

Surprisingly, the boy didn't give her an argument. He slipped out of his shoes, climbed onto the couch, and Hope covered him with a crocheted blanket. His dog hopped up and cuddled into his bent legs.

Hope found Mary in the kitchen making tea. "I need to go out to the barn to make a call. The man I fled from has found me. He's here."

Heart beating in his ears, Travis strode down the side of the house, sticking close for cover. He moved around back. He had the advantage here. This was his property. He had a woodpile stacked against a shed about fifty feet from the back of the house. He glanced to make sure the man hadn't come into the yard, then he made a break for it. He could set up behind the shed and make sure Derek couldn't escape out back.

What Travis gained in home-court advantage, he lost

because Derek was familiar with tactical moves. He, too, was in law enforcement.

Travis peered around the side of the shed and he spotted Derek inside the house, crossing in front of the back window. He was pacing. He had obviously been careful to stay clear of the front windows but had made a mistake in back. Travis squinted, hoping for some sign of Aiden and Hope. Where were they?

Derek was holding his head and animatedly talking and pointing. He seemed unhinged. Travis couldn't stand by and watch things unfold. People he cared about could be in imminent danger.

Travis checked to see if it was clear. Derek had moved out of the window. Travis stepped out from behind the safety of the shed and almost instantaneously the sound of breaking glass reached his ears and a shot zinged by his cheek. Travis dropped to the ground, then rolled behind the woodpile and aimed the rifle at the back window.

Adrenaline surged through his veins. He had underestimated Derek. Travis had thought he was distracted, but perhaps he had been putting on a show to draw Travis out.

Who knew?

Another shot split the wood to the right of him.

"Come out, Derek! No need to hurt anyone else," Travis called. Out of the corner of his eye, he noticed a couple deputies taking up positions in the shadows of the yard.

"No way! She's mine!" Derek shouted.

Travis didn't have to ask who "she" was.

"She thinks she can trade me for you?" Derek let out a menacing laugh. And in that instant, the spotlight over the back door popped on, illuminating Hope's ex and his automatic weapon. "Let's see who the better man is."

Derek lifted the weapon and the bullets rained down over Travis's head.

Sticking low to the ground, Travis scrambled behind the shed. He moved around the far side, but the way Derek was stalking across the yard, he must have thought Travis was still hunkered down behind the wood.

Travis steadied his aim and shot, hitting Derek center mass. The man spun toward him and a sly smile slanted his face.

Body armor.

Travis glanced behind him. The woods were his only hope of escape. Thankfully, he had always been fast. He heard a few more shots get off from his fellow deputies, but Wall was still advancing. Travis retreated to the woods.

When Derek reached the shed, he jerked and glanced around, obviously surprised no one was there.

The light from the house lit up Wall like an outline of a human target on the shooting range. Clearing his mind, Travis lifted the rifle and aimed at the man's head. Nothing less would do with his body armor. Travis squeezed the trigger and the man crumpled to the ground.

Travis swallowed hard and cautiously stepped out from behind a tree trunk. His fellow deputies ran in from either side, everyone with a gun at the ready.

"Pulse is weak." It was then that Travis realized it was the sheriff. The sheriff talked into his shoulder radio, demanding a bus.

Travis wasn't as optimistic. The man who had terrorized Hope was unconscious, blood oozing from his mouth.

"Rot in hell," Travis muttered, then he took off for the house. He had to find Aiden and Hope.

Another deputy caught up with him and stuck out his hand. "Let me go in."

Travis shot him a defiant glance. "No, I'm going in." It had been his job to keep Hope and Aiden safe. He had failed.

He stepped into his kitchen. The world seemed to move

in slow motion. The coffee pot still had the remnants of the coffee he had brewed this morning. A million years ago.

"Hope!" he called as he moved from the kitchen to the family room, his pulse thundering in his ears. "Aiden!" He stormed down the hallway and busted into the guest room. Empty.

He pivoted and checked the main bedroom, the closets, any place a petite woman and small boy could be held.

Or hide.

Doors opened and closed as the other deputies joined in the hunt.

"Travis," a deputy called, his tone urgent.

Travis turned and met the man in the kitchen.

"I got a call from dispatch. Your nephew and Hope Miller are with Mary Lapp at her bed-and-breakfast."

Thank you, God.

"They're okay and asking for you," the deputy said.

Travis pivoted and raced toward the door. "Tell them I'm on my way."

CHAPTER 22

Travis jumped out of the passenger seat of Deputy Flagler's patrol car. He bolted to the front door of the B&B without turning back.

Mary must have heard the vehicle because she was waiting at the door. Without him having to say anything, she said, "They're in here." She held out her hand.

Hope was sitting on the couch looking exhausted while Aiden was asleep next to her. Cujo used the boy's feet as his pillow.

Travis knelt in front of them and placed his hand on her knee and locked eyes with her, a well of emotions making it difficult to speak. He ran his hand over Aiden's head and leaned over and kissed him on the cheek. The child didn't even stir.

Travis felt a hand on his shoulder and he looked up to see Mary Lapp staring down at him. "A deputy is in the kitchen. Let me sit with the child."

Travis nodded. Hope scooted out from under Aiden and placed a pillow under his head.

Mary sat down in the rocker across from the couch. "I'll wait here in case he wakes up."

"I appreciate it," Hope whispered.

Travis led her to the kitchen with a hand to the small of her back. He wanted to pull her into a fierce embrace but sensed this wasn't the time or place. "Thank you for protecting him," he whispered into her hair.

Hope leaned into him slightly, then looked up with watery eyes. "I couldn't let anything happen to that sweet boy."

"Are you okay, ma'am?" Deputy Flagler asked.

Hope nodded. "Fine."

Travis ran his thumb across a cut on her cheek. Hope lifted her hand to where he had touched. "A tree branch. We had to run through the woods. I'm so glad he didn't follow us."

"It was probably too dark." Travis shrugged. "Who can guess? He was obviously unhinged."

"Would you be up for coming to the station to make a report?" the deputy asked.

"Could I bring her down in the morning?" Travis asked. "I think most of the loose ends are wrapped up. I'm sure it can wait."

Hope looked up at him, curiosity and concern in her eyes. "You arrested him?"

Caitlin touched Hope's hand. "I'll let you two talk." Then to Travis she said, "The sheriff will want an official report."

"Of course." Caitlin turned toward the door and Travis called after her. "Thanks, deputy."

She lifted her hand in a wave that suggested *No worries*.

After his fellow deputy stepped outside, Travis pulled Hope close. She wrapped her arms around him and squeezed. She rested her cheek on his chest and began to sob.

"It's over," he said into her hair. "Derek Wall is dead."

Hope froze, then pulled back a fraction to meet his gaze and uttered one single word. "How?"

Travis explained what happened and Hope stood there taking it in. Shell-shocked. She stared off in the middle distance. "I can go home now? I can stop looking over my shoulder." She swiped at tears falling silently down her cheeks. A slow smile tipped the corners of her mouth and she whispered, "I'm finally free."

"You're free," Travis repeated, then suddenly got a sinking feeling in his gut.

He wanted to get to know Hope better, and he wouldn't have that opportunity if she left Hunters Ridge. But he'd never tell her that. She had been through too much. He couldn't be selfish. He owed her for protecting his nephew.

"You can go home and feel safe, Hope."

"I suppose you can call me Harper now." She smiled, the relief evident on her face.

"Okay, Harper." Travis moved his hand in a circular motion on her back, comforting her.

Harper could have stayed in Travis's arms all night, but he probably needed to fill out paperwork, get Aiden settled... And check on his sister. All this had happened during one eventful night.

She lifted her head and kissed him on the cheek and stepped back, effectively breaking the spell. "How is your sister?"

Travis shook his head. In the dim kitchen, lit by the flickering kerosene lamp, the skin under his eyes looked sallow. "Not good," he whispered, as if holding on to his emotions by a thread. "They don't expect her to make it through the night."

"Oh, I'm so, so, so sorry," she said, unable to find any other words of comfort. Harper squared her shoulders. "Go and be with her. I'll take care of Aiden. I'm sure Mary won't mind if he sleeps in one of the guest rooms."

A look of hesitation flashed in his eyes.

"We'll be fine." Harper glanced to the window and could see the headlights from the deputy's patrol car in the driveway. "Go. It looks like the deputy is still here. I'm sure she could drive you back to the hospital."

Travis nodded, seemingly still not convinced, but he gave her a quick kiss on the forehead and turned on his heel. Before he reached the door, he said, "Tell Aiden I'll be back in the morning. Tell him I love him."

"Of course." Harper watched him leave, then went to find Mary and Aiden. "Is it okay if he sleeps in one of the guest rooms tonight?"

"*Yah.*"

Harper appreciated that the woman who kindly took her in didn't make a fuss that they'd have to redo the sheets where Aiden was about to sleep before the B&B guests arrived tomorrow. Harper lifted the boy and carried him upstairs. Cujo followed.

After she got him settled, she came back down, surprised to find Mary still up.

"I couldn't sleep," Mary said. She was sitting at the kitchen table with her hands placed flat over something Harper couldn't see.

"I don't think I'll sleep much either." Harper sat down in the chair across from the woman. Harper glanced toward the stairs. "Ada must sleep like a rock."

Mary laughed, but there was a sadness in her eyes.

"What's wrong?" Harper said, leaning forward and putting her hands over Mary's.

"Everything." Mary sniffed. "I couldn't help but overhear that Aiden's mother is gravely ill."

Harper nodded, not trusting her voice. After taking a few deep breaths, she said, "It's tough to lose a mom. I was twelve. I can't imagine only being five." She cleared her throat.

"Such a tragic thing," Mary said with a faraway quality to her voice.

"This whole night. Aiden and me running through the woods to get away from my ex. I'm sorry I brought my troubles to your doorstep. I should have never put you in danger."

Mary gave her a subtle nod and pressed her lips together.

"I suppose I should tell you my real name is Harper Miller. I'm sorry I lied, but I was afraid of my ex."

"And you're not afraid of him anymore?" Mary's intense stare unnerved her.

"He was killed." She still couldn't wrap her head around it. Tears prickled the back of her eyes. So many emotions. A man—a bad man—had lost his life. But still…

"I can't imagine what you've gone through," Mary said, keeping her hands neatly folded on the table.

"Thank you for providing me a job without asking me a lot of questions. You're a very good person."

Mary looked up and locked eyes with her. "I'm not." She sniffed. "I'm really not."

Harper pulled her hand away. "What is it?"

She could see Mary visibly swallow. She lifted her hands and turned over a photo. It was the photo of Mary, Harper and her mother the summer before her mother died, but it wasn't her copy.

"I don't understand." Harper felt her pulse rushing through her ears. "Why do you have a copy of that photo?"

"I lied to you, too." Mary ran the pad of her index finger

over the photo, tracing the outline of herself, then Harper. "I did know your mom. She mailed this to me."

Harper stayed silent, feeling like she was on the verge of learning something big. Something life-shattering.

"Your mom and I were friends. When I was eighteen, I went to Buffalo on *Rumspringa*. Your mom was a college student at the time and she had a little ad in the library that she was looking for a roommate." Mary bit her trembling lip. "You see, I had only gone to Buffalo initially for a weekend, but I met a boy. It's always a boy, isn't it? I made the uncharacteristic—for me anyway—spontaneous decision to stay. At least for a little while. I was smitten."

"You and my mom were roommates? Why wouldn't you tell me that? You said you didn't know her." A million jumbled thoughts scrambled around Harper's brain. She hadn't shared her real name with Mary when she initially showed her that photograph. Harper hadn't felt it necessary to expose herself, especially since the Amish woman claimed she hadn't remembered the photo or the woman in it.

Harper hadn't been the only one harboring secrets.

Mary held up a shaky hand. She seemed like the shell of the woman Harper had met less than two months ago. "Let me tell my story."

Harper nodded. She was able to hear each whoosh of her blood pulsing through her ears.

"Well, that boy I thought I loved left me as soon as he found out I was pregnant."

Harper grew lightheaded at the slow dawning and stars began to dance in her eyes.

"After I had the baby, I asked your mother if she could put it up for adoption. Your mother said that there were Safe Haven laws. That a baby could be left at a fire station, no questions asked. I was about to do it, then your mother said that she'd make sure the baby was truly safe." She turned the photo facedown on her lap and placed her hand over it again. "As soon as I was feeling well, I returned to Hunters Ridge, asked for forgiveness, got baptized and married. I never looked back. Of course, no one knew about the baby. That might have been a bridge too far."

"What happened to that baby?" Harper asked, her mouth going dry. She already knew the answer, but she had to hear it from Mary.

"I thought your mother was going to take it to the fire hall. Make sure the baby was safe until someone picked it up."

Mary's words conveyed distance, a disconnect. As if the baby hadn't come from her. "I don't know why she decided to raise the baby as her own. When she showed up here years ago with you, I realized what she had done. She had raised you herself. She came here to ask if I wanted to be part of your life. I was horrified. My husband...I don't know what he would have done. I had to protect my family. The life I had built." Mary's shoulders dropped and she buried her face in her hands. "Don't you see, I had no choice?"

Harper stared at Mary—her birth mother—who had just revealed her biggest secret. Harper couldn't find any words.

"Your mother never mentioned being sick. If I had known..."

"Would you have done anything differently if you had known?" Harper asked, gaining some steel in her spine. "*Could you* have done anything different?"

Mary looked her dead in the eyes. "I don't know."

Not wanting to say something she'd regret, Harper stood on wobbly legs and went upstairs. She got ready for bed and climbed in. A headache pounded behind her eyes and she couldn't turn off her brain. Mary Lapp was her mother. The woman who she had thought was her mother had decided to raise her when asked to surrender her to a Safe Haven drop box.

Why? Why? Why?

At some point, Harper fell asleep and woke up to loud voices downstairs. She threw on jeans and a T-shirt and went down to find Travis, Aiden, and Ada—*my half-sister*—having breakfast. Mary had prepared pancakes and fresh fruit.

"Are you hungry?" Mary asked with a hopeful look in her eyes. When Harper didn't answer, the woman pressed. "You should eat."

"Thank you," Harper said out of politeness, and sat down.

"I'm going to have Aiden gather up his things," Travis said, then ushered his nephew out of the kitchen.

"I'll give you a hand," Ada said.

Harper looked over at Mary—her mother—at the stove. "All this time you knew I was Harper Miller and not Hope Baker?"

Mary slid into the chair next to Harper's. "I had my own secrets." Mary squeezed her hand. "I'd love to start over, if we could."

This had probably been what her mother had wanted, long before Mary was ready to accept her daughter back into her life. Harper smiled. "I'd like that." Despite an undercurrent of hurt, in that moment, Harper made a conscious decision to forgive her birth mother. Mary had been under tremendous stress, yet in the end, she had taken Harper in when she truly needed her.

"Will you stick around a bit?"

Harper had no real reason to leave and a lot of reasons to stay, including the man in the other room. "I'd like that."

After breakfast, Ada taught Aiden how to play jacks which quickly became a game of keep-away with Cujo. Harper was nursing her coffee at the kitchen table when Travis came in. "Have a minute?"

"Sure."

Travis reached out and took her hand. "Come outside with me." He led her to the rocking chairs and they sat down.

"What is it?" Harper asked, feeling the warm and fuzzies from earlier slipping away. "Is it your sister?"

Travis nodded and his eyes grew red rimmed. He cleared his throat. "Ginny passed at three this morning."

She stood and placed her hand on his shoulder, albeit a little awkwardly. "I'm so, so sorry."

Travis reached up and covered her hand. "Yeah, me too."

She glanced toward the house where sounds of Aiden and Ada giggling over their game could be heard. "Aiden doesn't know."

"I'll tell him when we go home. I haven't had the heart."

"What's going to happen to him?" she whispered, thinking about herself as the little baby who almost ended up in a box at the firehouse.

"He has a father." Travis didn't sound too thrilled by the prospect. "Kerry's out on bail."

Harper nodded, unsure of what to say next. How would that sweet little boy do living with a drug addict? Again.

"The county will get involved. Make sure he has a clean place to live." Travis stood up and her hand fell from his shoulder. "I'll stay on top of things, too. Aiden will not fall through the cracks."

"He's lucky to have you in his life."

Travis's lips flattened into a thin line. "Are you sticking around for a while?"

"For a bit." She was still trying to process the fact that Mary was her biological mother. She had lost the only other mother she knew and she wasn't about to leave without exploring this new relationship.

"Good. Maybe after things settle, I can take you out on a proper date." He reached over and squeezed her hand, then he frowned. "I must sound tacky asking you on a date on the same day my sister died."

"You're dealing with a lot of emotions. Take care of your family. I promise I'll still be in town when it's the right time."

He took her hand and pressed the back of it to his lips. "Thanks."

Harper furrowed her brow. "For what?"

"For giving me something to look forward to on one of the worst days of my life." He let out a long shuddering breath.

Harper took a step closer and wrapped her arms around his midsection and placed her head on his solid chest. He returned the embrace and she closed her eyes, sharing in this man's grief. For the first time in a long time, she felt safe and secure in the arms of a man.

"We'll get through this together," she whispered into his chest.

CHAPTER 23

A week later, rain hit the green tent over the final resting place of Virginia "Ginny" Turner *wife, mom, sister, daughter.* The weather provided the perfect mood for one of the worst days in Travis's life. Next to him sat his mother, grim faced and holding her clasped hands tightly in her lap. On the other side of her sat Aiden with his father, Kerry.

The minister had finished saying the prayers and Travis shifted to pick up a white rose to lay on the casket when he noticed Harper standing toward the back with her head bowed. They had met for coffee three times this past week. She had been enormously helpful as a sounding board for Ginny's burial plans, for dealing with Kerry, and simply listening. She hadn't however, said she was going to attend his sister's funeral.

Travis had found himself truly falling for her, but he wanted to be respectful of her space and her need to heal. She had just gotten out of an abusive relationship and could finally breathe. He didn't want to crowd her. And he'd let her know that.

Travis turned his attention back to the casket. Kerry looked frail and shaky, probably going through withdrawal. He held his son's hand and the pair of them placed their roses on the casket of their wife and mother. Travis let out a long breath between tight lips. No kid should have to lose their mom at this age.

He guided his own mother to the casket of her only daughter. His mother kissed a rose then tossed it on the casket. *Rest In Peace, Ginny.* Travis tossed his rose.

As the ceremony ended, the attendees mingled, giving their condolences before dispersing to their vehicles, one or two to an umbrella. His mother was engaged in conversation with a few women from her church. These same women had been a great source of comfort to her, probably more so than he had.

Travis found himself searching the faces for Harper, and an overwhelming sense of comfort washed over him when he saw her approaching.

She leaned in close and smelled of cucumbers and rain. "How are you holding up?" she whispered, sliding her hand around the crook of his arm.

Travis patted her cool hand. "I'm doing better now." When they weren't meeting over coffee, they were exchanging texts and phone calls. He felt like they were having a crash course on getting to know one another.

Harper raised up onto her tippy-toes and gave him a kiss on the cheek. "You've been in my prayers."

His heart warmed. "Thank you." He squeezed her hand. "I do have good news. Deputy Johnny Lehman is expected to make a full recovery. I got a call from his brother this morning."

"That is good news. I felt so awful he got hurt while trying to protect me." Harper shook her head. "That is good news," she repeated, her relief palpable.

Out of the corner of his eye he saw Aiden break free from his father, who was talking to someone who seemed rail thin and disheveled. Sadly, probably another user. His nephew made a beeline to Harper and flung his arms around her waist and buried his head into her belly.

"Oh honey," Harper said, running her hand over his head.

Kerry, dressed in a black trench coat that was both too broad and too long, strolled over to them, curling a piece of paper in his hands nervously.

Harper was the first one to speak. "Sorry for your loss."

Travis admired how she was able to overlook the fact that Kerry had nearly killed her when he had plowed his car through the front of the Wash & Go. The accident had happened less than a month ago, but it felt like a lifetime.

Kerry nodded. He had always seemed awkward in social situations. "I wanted to talk to you, Travis," he mumbled.

"Okay." Travis waited expectantly, not moving out from under the protection of the tent. The rain had picked up and they'd get drenched when they crossed the cemetery for their cars. "Should we step away?" He tipped his chin toward his nephew. Perhaps this wasn't a conversation for little ears.

"No, I've already talked to him." Kerry reached out to touch his son but dropped his hand short of making contact. "I...um...was wondering if you guys could watch Aiden. I mean...just until...and he has fun with you guys and all..." Kerry tried to string the words together to make his request. Perhaps he was going to make a solid effort to get clean. Or maybe he didn't want the responsibility of being a single parent.

Travis decided he wasn't going to press him on any of this in front of his nephew. "I'd love to have him," he said. "Whatever you need." He couldn't speak for Harper. She was probably going back to Buffalo at some point, however he wished more than anything that she'd stay.

"Aiden and I have become great friends," Harper said. The child was still clinging to her. "Right, buddy?" She angled her head to look at his face. Aiden looked up and opened his palm to show her the blue worry stone.

Kerry ran his hand roughly over his hair, leaving it in messy tufts. "Thanks, thanks. Um...maybe you could take him now. I could drop stuff off later." Without waiting for confirmation, Kerry tapped on his son's back with a long index finger. "Hey, you're going to go home with Uncle Travis and Aunt Harper just like we talked about."

Aiden slowly released his grip on Harper and looked up pleadingly at his dad. "Where are you going?"

"I got stuff to do." A pained expression rippled across the man's face.

Harper crouched down and lifted the boy up. "You'll hang out with us, okay? Maybe we can play a board game."

Aiden nodded and tucked his head under her chin. He was getting a bit big to be carried, but he had been through a lot. Travis took the boy from Harper, and after seeing that his mother was going to get home with some of her church friends, they walked across the lawn to his truck together.

Under her purple umbrella Harper shrugged. "Little Amos dropped me off in Mary's rental van. I figured I could get a ride back with you."

He smiled. "Hop in."

After he buckled Aiden in the back seat—he had finally picked up a booster for him—he climbed into the driver's side and glanced over at Harper. They had all been through a lot together in a short time. And he was grateful they had one another. He figured he'd take each day as it came—the tragedy of his sister's death reminded him how short life was —and it seemed Harper Miller was looking to do the same.

hristmas morning...

Harper woke up early and headed downstairs at the B&B. She flipped the switch for the beautiful white lights on the Christmas tree. Cujo lifted his head then set it back down, apparently not ready to leave his cozy bed in the corner of the room. Even though most Amish weren't big on Christmas decorations, Mary—Harper still called her biological mother "Mary"—had an oversized live Christmas tree set up in the sitting room. When Mary had the generator installed for electricity for her guests, she had probably not considered bright white lights adorning a tree, but here they were.

Last year at this time, Harper had still been in Buffalo, worried about making everything perfect so Derek wouldn't find a reason to punch her upside the head. She remembered making a wish on a star that she'd find a way out. She had been desperate.

And now, here she was...

Old name. Old hair color. Better life.

Much better life.

What a difference a year had made.

Harper and Mary had grown close over the past few months, but out of respect for Mary and her place in the Amish community, they had decided to keep their true relationship secret. Harper understood and accepted that. She also came to understand why Mary hadn't wanted to acknowledge Harper as her daughter when her mother came to visit the summer before she died. It would have thrown Mary's entire life—and that of her children—into upheaval.

Mary claimed she hadn't realized how truly sick Harper's mother was, and she also naively thought that someone might reach out to her if something did indeed happen to her. Of course, there was no way that could have happened because no one knew that Mary existed. And Mary never knew Harper's father's last name, so there was no way of tracking him down. And quite frankly, Harper didn't feel a need to. So now the women worked side by side every day, enjoying their newfound relationship.

"You're up early," Mary said, sitting down in the rocking chair next to hers. "The tree looks beautiful."

"It's the prettiest one I've ever seen."

"I've never done a Christmas quite like this one."

There was a heap of presents under the tree, mostly toys for Aiden. But the child had probably received the best present earlier this week when his uncle was able to officially adopt him, providing a stable home. Things had moved quickly through the courts after Kerry willingly gave up all his rights. The man had made one unselfish choice in his life.

Harper had made sure there were a few gifts for Ada and Mary without offending them by appearing too materialistic and thus not in the true spirit of Christmas. "Thank you for letting us celebrate here. It seemed the easiest way to gather everyone together." Travis and Aiden were sharing one of the guest rooms, and of course, the three women had their own rooms.

Mary leaned over and playfully tapped the back of her daughter's hand. "We wouldn't want tongues wagging now, would we?"

Harper laughed. Nothing could ruin today. She had only blessings to count.

Mary slid to the edge of the rocker and stood. She grabbed an envelope off the oak table. "This came for you yesterday."

Harper opened the card and found a beautiful photo of Miss June and Skylar decorating cookies at the nursing home, with a little note scribbled on the bottom: *Can't wait to see you in the new year!* Harper smiled and tucked the card in the envelope. It felt wonderful to have friends back in her life.

Footsteps pounding down the stairs drew their attention. Harper turned to see Aiden, his hair all mussed, standing in his footed Christmas PJ's, wide-eyed and happy. "Santa came! Santa came!" He spun on the slippery feet of the PJ's. "I'm going to wake up Uncle Travis and Ada. Tell them Santa was here."

Mary and Harper locked gazes and smiled. It was about time that child experienced joy.

A few minutes later Ada came downstairs, fully dressed in her plain clothes, followed by Travis in casual sweats and a T-shirt that accentuated his broad chest. Cujo sprang out of his dog bed to greet Travis, probably his favorite person after Aiden. Why wouldn't he be, considering the man spoiled the dog.

"Merry Christmas," Travis said, his voice deep from just waking up.

"Merry Christmas," Harper and Mary said in unison.

"Santa outdid himself," Ada said, deadpan. She was far too old to be looking for something from Santa, but because she didn't grow up with the tradition, she viewed it with fresh, child-like eyes.

"I think you'll find some things from Santa to you, Ada," Harper said.

"Really?" The young woman pressed her clasped hands to her chest.

Hearing that, Aiden dropped to his knees and sounded out the names on the gift tags. He pulled out a box decorated in pretty Santa wrap and handed it to Ada. "This one has your name on it."

With pure delight, she unwrapped the gift to find a leather-bound journal and colored gel pens. Harper had noticed her journaling on a drugstore spiral notebook. This would be a fancy improvement. "I love it," Ada said, as she ran her hand across the cover.

Aiden got back down on all fours and rooted around the back of the tree. He emerged a second time with a small box. "Hey! This one is for Aunt Harper from Uncle Travis."

Travis jumped up from his spot on the steps. "Um, I was going to save that for later."

Harper cut him a curious gaze.

Ignoring him, Aiden plopped the gift on her lap. "Here, open it."

"Oh…" Harper's cheeks burned hot. "I think I'll wait." Then she looked up at Travis, her heart beating wildly in her chest. "I thought we agreed not to exchange gifts."

He pressed his lips together and raised his eyebrows.

"Come on now," Ada said, suddenly invested in the scene

playing out in front of her. "You can't make someone wait to open a gift. That's not fair."

"That's right," Mary said, joining in. "What about the spirit of Christmas?"

"I'm sure if Travis wants to wait…" Nervous butterflies flitted in her belly. What could possibly be in this small box?

It couldn't be? Could it?

Travis came over to her and ran his hand through his hair. "Seems everyone has spoken. You need to open it."

With trembling hands Harper tore open the giftwrap.

Travis gently took the black box from her hands and got down on one knee. He opened the box, revealing a gorgeous diamond solitaire. "Will you marry me, Harper Miller?"

"Yes!" Happy tears sprang from her eyes. She held out her hand, and he slipped the ring on her finger then swept her up in a huge embrace.

"I hadn't planned on proposing in my PJ's." He laughed. "I had plans to get dressed and go for a snowy walk and propose under the stars tonight," he whispered in her ear.

She lifted her hand between them and stared at the gorgeous ring. "It's beautiful. This is perfect."

"You know why I wanted to propose under the stars?"

Harper shook her head.

"Because when you offered to show Aiden the Big Dipper, I saw how kind and compassionate you are, and it was then that I knew we were going to have a future together."

Harper looked up at him. "That was the night we first met. The night…" She left out the accident and finding Aiden huddled among the heaps of garbage while his mom was unconscious. "You knew then?"

"Let's just say that I had high hopes." He pressed his lips to hers and smiled.

"Gross!" Aiden hollered, then rolled over on his back and grabbed his knees and giggled.

Harper pressed her left hand to her chest, her engagement ring sparkling under the white Christmas tree lights.

Ada and Mary came over to admire her ring and to offer their congratulations. "I was right when I said I'd never had a Christmas quite like this one." Mary smiled and tugged Ada's hand. "Let's go get coffee and cinnamon buns and then we can watch Aiden open the rest of his presents from Santa."

Aiden followed the two women into the kitchen, asking if he could lick the frosting spoon.

Travis pulled Harper into another embrace, pressing his body to hers. "I love you. I can't wait to spend the rest of our lives together."

"I love you, too." Harper couldn't wait, but mostly she was happy to live in the moment, at peace.

Sometimes the best gifts were things you couldn't put under a tree. She looked down at her sparkling ring again. However, these kinds of things were nice, too, especially when they came from the right person.

Filled with joy, Harper plopped down on the couch and pulled Travis down next to her. She wrapped her left hand around his bicep, unable to tear her gaze from the new ring on her finger. "I hope you still plan on taking me for a walk under the stars tonight."

Travis leaned over and kissed her forehead. "Tonight and every night after that. Of course, if that's what you'd like to do."

Harper pressed her cheek against his arm. "I don't care what we do, as long as it's together."

Dear Reader,

I hope you enjoyed **Plain Trouble**. *If you're looking for something else to read, please check out my "Also by..." page in* *this book. Or perhaps I can recommend* Pointe & Shoot, *a cozy mystery set in the competitive dance world. I like to call it my* Blue Bloods *meets* Dance Moms *book. Competition can be killer...*

Happy reading 🩶,
Alison

ABOUT THE AUTHOR

Alison Stone is a **Publishers Weekly bestselling author** who writes sweet romance, cozy mysteries, and inspirational romantic suspense, some of which contain bonnets and buggies.

Alison often refers to herself as the "accidental Amish author." She decided to try her hand at the genre after an editor put a call out for more Amish romantic suspense. Intrigued—and who doesn't love the movie *Witness* with Harrison Ford?—Alison dug into research, including visits to the Amish communities in Western New York where she lives. This sparked numerous story ideas, the first leading to her debut novel with Harlequin Love Inspired Suspense. Four subsequent Love Inspired Suspense titles went on to earn **RT magazine's TOP PICK!** designation, their highest ranking.

When Alison's not plotting ways to bring mayhem to Amish communities, she's writing romantic suspense with a more modern setting, sweet romances, and cozy mysteries. In order to meet her deadlines, she has to block the internet and hide her smartphone.

Married and the mother of four (almost) grown kids, Alison lives in the suburbs of Buffalo where the summers are gorgeous and the winters are perfect for curling up with a book—or writing one.

Be the first to learn about new books, giveaways and deals in Alison's newsletter. Sign up at AlisonStone.com.

Connect with Alison Stone online:

www.AlisonStone.com

Alison@AlisonStone.com

ALSO BY ALISON STONE

The Thrill of Sweet Suspense Series

(Stand-alone novels that can be read in any order)

Random Acts

Too Close to Home

Critical Diagnosis

Grave Danger

The Art of Deception

Hunters Ridge: Amish Romantic Suspense

Plain Obsession: Book 1

Plain Missing: Book 2

Plain Escape: Book 3

Plain Revenge: Book 4

Plain Survival: Book 5

Plain Inferno: Book 6

Plain Trouble: Book 7

A Jayne Murphy Dance Academy Cozy Mystery

Pointe & Shoot

Final Curtain

For a complete list of books visit

Alison Stone's Amazon Author Page

Made in United States
North Haven, CT
21 April 2022

18453548R00104